6-8-99

DEATH IN EXILE

Laurel Schunk

St Kitts Press
Wichita, Kansas

PUBLISHED BY ST KITTS PRESS
A division of S-K Publications
PO Box 8173
Wichita, KS 67208
1-888-705-4887 (toll-free)
316-685-3201
FAX 316-685-6650
stkitts@skpub.com
www.skpub.com/stkitts/

The name St Kitts and its logo are registered trademarks.

This novel is a work of fiction. Any references to real people
and places are used only to give a sense of reality. All of the
characters are the product of the author's imagination, as
are their thoughts, actions, motivations, or dialog. Any re-
semblance to real people and events is purely coincidental.

Edited by Elizabeth Whiteker
Cover design by Diana Tillison

ISBN 0-9661879-2-X
Library of Congress Catalog Card Number: 98-86628
Copyright © 1998 by Laurel Schunk

First Edition 1998

CHAPTER 1

Martha Mathers was miffed. She was not guilty of the allegation that man had made about her. She'd been housekeeper for Lady Diana Atwood and her parents for nigh on thirty years, from well before Lady Diana was born, and while Lady Diana hadn't accused her, her beast of a husband had.

It wasn't just the slur against her good name. It was also the fact that he refused to give her a character. So now she was without a livelihood, and worse, without the pension she had been promised for her old age. It was unjust, that's what it was!

So here she sat slaving over the letter to the lady. It wasn't easy for her to write a whole letter— a household shopping list, that was different.

She smoothed back her neat salt and pepper hair above a thin, lined face, with its large black eyes. She'd always been told she had fine eyes, and she guessed she did, but that didn't seem important in life.

Schunk

My lady, she wrote with a long, slim hand, the fingers beginning to cramp and gnarl from rheumatism, *I know you're havin a hard time of it yourself right now, but I beg of you, lady, in your parents' honor, gie me a character so I can find a position.*

If not, I'll have to talk to the judge, as I told your Mr. Rutledge I would. I hate to do it, but I canna live now without a position or the pension your late father promised me.

She picked up her wadded-up handkerchief and wiped her eyes. A sad day it was.

She finished the letter, then signed and folded it; at that point she heard a soft knock at the cottage door where she was spending two weeks with her sister. Her sister was gone for the day at market in the next town, so Mrs. Mathers had to answer it herself.

She put the letter into its envelope and carried it to the door. She opened it to the man who'd carried her valise to the coach stop after she had been shown the door.

He bowed. "Mrs. Mathers. I was concerned about you and wondered how you were doing in your search for a place."

"Oh, not good at all, sir," she said, blinking back tears his sympathy had called up. She wiped at the corners of her eyes. "It's good of you to ask."

"I wanted to know because I've heard of a place you may want to ask for. It's as housekeeper for my uncle, near Dover. I thought I would leave you his name and address so you can write him."

Relief flooded over her, and she smiled. "Oh, you are kind, sir! Won't you come in and I'll take the address from you."

He bowed slightly and gestured for her to proceed him. Once he closed the door behind him, he reached out and put a kid-gloved hand on her shoulder. "Mrs. Mathers?" he said softly.

When she turned to face him, he grabbed her by the throat and choked her until her face, empurpled and swollen, signaled life was gone, and he let her dead body fall to the floor. He leaned across her to reach the letter crumpled in her hand. He removed it from the envelope and read it quickly, then stuffed it in his pocket. He crossed to the table where she'd been obviously composing this potentially troublesome missive, where he looked for anything else that might be incriminating.

Nothing. That was good.

Next he took a slim rope from another pocket and strung the pathetic, slight woman up from the kitchen rafter and arranged a chair on the floor, as if it had been knocked over.

Upon surveying his work, he dusted off his hands, smiled, and nonchalantly strode out of the house. She certainly didn't have to worry about a pension for her old age now, did she?

Schunk

Anna Katherine Elizabeth Forsythe walked briskly along Bond Street. The crisp fall weather put color in her cheeks and a light dance in her step. Although November, it was a lovely day, all blue and golden.

Amazingly, she had been able to slip away alone this morning. Aunt Lydia was preoccupied with Anna's charges, who were Lydia's grandchildren. Lydia was happy to be needed while her daughter-in-law Constance was alone, with Lydia's son, Ansten Stanfield, Lord Cadogan, off soldiering in Canada—so Anna Kate was on her own.

Along the way, she nodded to people who smiled and bobbed in greeting to her. She knew she looked quite fine in her rose velvet carriage dress. It set off the damask rose of her skin. While she wasn't vain—Papa would be horrified if she displayed any such failing—she knew that rose brought out the best in her coloring, with her big slate blue eyes and warm golden brown hair. And her new rose velvet muff and bonnet trimmed in white fur made her feel the height of fashion.

Though her father, vicar in the villages of Breckin and Andover, feared she would become vain, she knew he was pleased with his only daughter's appearance. He called her "wholesome" rather than beautiful, but she knew in her heart he was proud of her.

Death in Exile

The plock-plock of horses' hooves, the rumble of carts and carriages, the rise and fall of voices in the streets all added to her sense of pleasure this bright morning. It was perhaps the first really joyful time she'd had since arriving in London. She was alone—as alone as a person could be on a market day in the largest city in the world—for the first time in months, with no one talking to her, asking for this or that, demanding her attention. It was lovely.

She chided herself for her self-pitying thoughts: Constance and Aunt Lydia treated her as well as family. Once again she felt ashamed for her negative emotions, which were certainly not socially acceptable among the Quality. But she didn't stay ashamed for long: she never could hold onto negative thoughts.

Yet her position as governess for Aunt Lydia's grandchildren was one of those mixed blessings she was the frequent recipient of: necessary for an impecunious young woman but so tiring and maddening for a proud one used to ordering her own life.

"Dear Papa," she whispered, "I miss you so. I'll be home by Christmas."

A voice startled her out of her reverie.

"Anna! Anna Kate!"

Anna Kate turned at the sound of that beloved voice. "Diana, is it you?"

Rushing toward her, having pushed through the throng of Friday shoppers, Diana Jane Atwood fell into her childhood friend's arms upon reaching her.

Anna Kate hugged Diana and cried, "It is wonderful to see you. I have missed you so!" She then held the tall, rake-thin girl back at arm's length to get a good look at her. "Diana, what is wrong?"

Diana's face looked gray and drawn. She threw herself into Anna Kate's arms and began to sob. "Anna, oh, Anna. What a blessed sight you are!" She cried herself out, then stepped away from her friend. Dipping her head in shame, she fumbled in the sleeve of her over-washed, thin cotton dress for a handkerchief. Over the dress she wore a thin sweater, nothing heavy enough for the weather.

Why was her wealthy friend not in silks or satins? She would not ask now, considering the crowds of people. Most merely rushed on past, ignoring the two. Others, too many for Anna's taste, stared. Putting her arm around Diana, she led her down the street to a small millinery shop. "Let's go in here to talk a bit. I'm sure Madame Veronique will not mind."

Anna Kate led Diana into the shop and then to a slipper chair covered in a forest green brocade. Diana looked as though she folded herself in half, gently like egg whites, as she eased into the chair.

"Are you in pain?" Anna whispered.

Diana shook her head, but tears started in her large gray eyes. "Come close, Anna Kate," she whispered.

"What is it?"

Death in Exile

Diana reached inside the bodice of her dress. Handing Anna Kate a black velvet pouch, stitched around all four edges, she said. "Please keep this safe for me. You'll never know how important it is."

Anna felt small and large lumps inside the velvet case, as well as long strands of some hard substance—chains and precious stones? "But what—? Oh, Diana, I will do my best." She stuck the bag into her muff.

"I need to tell you. Rutledge has killed Mathers—"

"Your housekeeper? But why?"

"To get at me. And there's no proof she was killed. He made it look like suicide, but it can't be. There's no way, with her deep religious faith, there's just no way." She put her hand up to hold her head. "My head hurts so much."

Anna Kate then noticed blood seeping through the thin dress, under Diana's left arm. "You're injured! I'll be right back." Keeping one eye on Diana, Anna stepped briskly behind a long curtain, also in green, that separated the front display room from the sewing room behind.

"Madame Vero, please come! My friend is injured!"

A tall, slim woman, with titian hair piled on top of her head, rose regally from the chair where she had been putting the finishing touches on a midnight blue turban. "O, la, what is the problem?" She bustled out of the back room and across to where Diana sat sideways on the chair.

Diana smiled weakly at the tall woman who stood before her with such royal bearing. "I...I will try not to bleed on your chair. Please forgive me..." She struggled to stand, but she fainted.

"Diana!" The skirts of Anna's rose velvet dress pooled around her as she quickly knelt beside her friend. "What should I do?" she asked the older woman.

Madame leaned over the still form and brushed the back of her hand across Diana's brow. "Burning with fever." She straightened. "Miss Forsythe, run for Blaine—that is, Mr. Sumner—down the next street. This young woman is very ill."

Anna smoothed the wheat-blond hair back from Diana's forehead, then nodded. "I'll be right back." She hated to leave her friend with someone Diana did not know, but Madame Vero was reliable.

She dashed out of the store, then, once on the street, slowed her pace to a more decorous speed. She kept her hands inside her muff to keep them from betraying her agitation. She touched the pouch Diana had given her—what had happened to Diana?

The last time she'd seen Diana was perhaps eighteen months ago at Papa's manse at home. Diana had just reached her twenty-second birthday and was due to inherit her grandfather's wealth. Anna remembered the lovely, elegant Diana, with her thick, shining wheat-blond hair, gray eyes, and clear porcelain skin. She always had a regal bearing Anna Kate knew was lacking in herself.

The clatter of hooves behind her roused her from her reverie. "Miss Forsythe!"

She turned to see a tall, muscular man approaching on a large black stallion. "Lord Wentworth!" Should she speak to him of Diana? But no, she decided perhaps she should listen first to see what Quillen Allyn Rossiter, fourth earl of Wentworth, and another childhood friend, would tell her.

"Have you seen Jane Atwood?" he asked brusquely.

"Jane Atwood?" she repeated.

"Yes, Jane. Surely you haven't forgotten—you were best of friends. Have you seen her?"

His haste shocked her, almost enough to make her blurt out something revealing, but she didn't want to disclose Diana's whereabouts without knowing why he searched for her. One fact puzzled her. Why was he calling her Jane? As children playing together, Diana was Diana, never Jane.

Quill. He had changed about three years ago. From being her chum he'd become an aloof adult. Once he'd come into his inheritance, he'd left her and their idyllic childhood behind. At one point she thought he was going to offer for her in marriage, but then he turned cold and distant.

She'd heard he'd taken to gambling and horse racing, much to his parents' dismay. Then, when his father died within the next year, Quill had had to step into his new position as earl, and as a result, he turned his back on his wild, wastrel days. She had heard he'd even taken his seat in the House of Lords. In any event, he'd moved out of her circle for good.

Anna ducked her chin and took a deep breath. "I regret, milord, I do not know where she is." Inside her muff she crossed two fingers on her right hand. She would have to confess lying later, in her bedtime prayers. "I haven't seen her for, oh, nearly two years." That statement would have been accurate twenty minutes ago.

Quill Rossiter swung down off his horse to approach her closely. Anna noted the black hair falling down over his eyes, the nearly black eyes under well-shaped brows. When he came close, she could smell his bay rum after-shave. He struck her as being very clean for a person hot in pursuit of her poor, injured friend. "I mean to say Diana, not Jane. Jane is what her husband calls her." He nearly spat the word *husband* out.

Anna was shocked by the venom in his voice. "What do you mean?"

"She was arrested for stealing Rutledge's family jewels and then running off," he said. "He's known as the Beast by all who know him, and he's been keeping her as a virtual prisoner for the last few months. I understand he has severely mistreated her. He's probably had her old family housekeeper murdered."

10

"Mathers? But why?"

He didn't answer, merely waved her interruption away. "Servants' gossip spread the tale that Rutledge fired the old family retainers, then that Rutledge's bailiff was bringing her to Newgate when she escaped."

"Newgate? Diana to prison! But why?"

"I just told you," Quill said crossly. "She has been accused of absconding with the family jewels, by her husband, her legal guardian. If you haven't seen her, just tell me. I must find her before Rutledge's man does. Rutledge has probably already killed once."

Anna examined his face carefully. When they were children together, so many years ago, Quillen Allyn Rossiter of Wentworth had been noted for his probity and honor. "And...and is she guilty?" she asked.

"Guilty? What are you saying, Anna! I'm surprised at you. Do you really believe Diana could ever...?"

By now he was shouting and drawing unwanted attention from passersby. "Shh," she said, "follow me. I must find a doctor."

"Anna Kate, I haven't time!" he thundered at her.

"Please," she said as gently as she could, "please come with me. I'll take you to her. But she's injured and very ill. I must fetch the doctor for her, milord."

11

Schunk

Quill's eyebrows rose. "You're hiding her? And no 'milording' me. I'm the same old Quill."

"Yes—Quill," she said. "At least thankfully you're no longer shouting. I suppose one could say I am hiding her. As I said, she is ill, and wounded."

"But, Anna, you must be very careful. If Rutledge finds out..."

She took a deep breath, then spoke as deliberately as she could, through clenched teeth. She began to walk away, hoping he would keep close. "Milord—Quill—I am beginning to lose my temper. If you stand here arguing in the street, Rutledge's man is very likely to find us, and through us, Diana. I beseech you, come!"

Quill nodded, then began following her, the stallion close behind. "Back, Brutus." The horse flung his head up and snorted as though he'd taken offense at his master's words. "He is young and has no manners."

Anna didn't reply. Instead she turned in at the next house, which boasted a brass plate by the door, *Surgery, Mr. Blaine Sumner.* She rang the bell while thinking the door, once cherry red, could use a new coat of paint. The brass needed a good polishing too.

She turned with a scowl for Quill and his mount. "That horse is nearly stepping on my heels. You're not planning on bringing the beast inside, are you?"

"You don't think I should? Do I not remember

a Miss Anna Kate Forsythe being the ringleader when the four of us brought two ponies and three lambs into the Manor?" By "the four of us" he meant himself, Anna, Lucas Cranford, and Diana, four childhood chums.

She blushed. "Hush. That was years ago. I'm much too old for such nonsense now."

He grinned at her. "Is that why you're hiding a thief and a runaway? Are you sure it is much different from the time you took those young hogs into the vicarage to keep them from being slaughtered?"

Anna put one hand up to her face. She knew it was beet red. "Oh, my, I had quite forgotten the hogs. But they had been such darling piglets..."

The door to the surgery opened. A middle-aged man with gray hair sprouting in all points of a compass at once stood before them. His small black eyes, beady under bushy gray brows, bored into her. "Well?" he barked.

"You are the doctor, Mr. Sumner?" Anna asked, still confused, caught as she was between the remembrances of her childhood escapades and Diana's situation.

The man pointed to the plate beside the door. "That's what it says, missy. What do you want?"

His gruffness helped bring Anna to her senses. She realized his clothing was in as poor a state as the door, the brass plate, and his eyebrows. "Oh, my," she whispered.

"Well, out with it, young lady! I'm a busy man."

"It's my friend...no, my scullery maid. She's had an accident or she's sick."

"Well, which is it?"

Her mouth dropped open, but she quickly recovered herself. "I don't know! She's injured and she has a fever. Oh, please, Mr. Sumner, won't you come? Madame Vero said you would."

He huffed through a shaggy mustache. "Hmph. Wait right here. I need to get my bag."

He shut the door in their faces. Anna turned to face Quill. "He is rather disreputable looking, is he not?" She stuck the hand she had used to ring the bell back into her muff to hide its tell-tale clenching and clutched the pouch inside it. She certainly did not want the fourth earl of Wentworth to know just how fretful she felt at this moment—nor that she was hiding something for Diana.

Quill smiled in a kindly fashion. "Doesn't mean a thing. He could be the best or the worst surgeon in the nation. You cannot tell by looking." He smoothed the black mane on the patient stallion. "Good old Brutus."

"You talk to that horse as though he is a dog or a child. Surely he does not understand you?"

"Of course he does. Brutus, bow to the lady."

Anna Kate smothered a giggle when the horse obeyed. What would Papa say, her giggling on the street? And besides, how could she? Diana was in grave, grave trouble.

CHAPTER 2

Anna Kate led the two men and the horse back to Mme Veronique's shop. She couldn't decide whether she should tell the doctor the truth or dissimulate.

She didn't need to worry, for Quill took charge of the situation. "Mr. Sumner," Quill said, "we have a delicate situation here. The young woman we need you to treat is running from the direst circumstance. I pray we can count on your discretion."

"I do know about professional ethics, young man. Now if you would get out of my way, I will look at this young friend or scullery maid for you." Anna could hear the doubt in his voice as he quoted her earlier words.

The doctor nearly strong-armed Quill, who gave place with a wink to Anna Kate. Sumner nodded perfunctorily to Mme Vero. Anna thought a secret smile passed between the two older people. Elegant Mme Vero and this awful, boorish little man? Whatever would she see in him?

Mr. Sumner scowled at Anna and Quill. "You two need to leave the room, now!"

Somehow the man's rudeness put Anna's mind at ease. Could a dishonorable person with such manners make it as a doctor? She doubted it.

Anna waved Quill into Mme Veronique's back room, where the fine, jewel-toned creations bound for ladies' heads were made. "Tell me how everyone at home is doing." She placed her muff, velvet pouch hidden inside, on a small table nearby and began removing her bonnet and cloak. She consciously mimicked the gracious moves of the upper class. She smiled at him, with one of those mannerly smiles she had seen on the faces of many of the ladies of the *ton*.

He stiffened, she thought, reacting as though he'd been struck. His next words shocked her, so different were they from the earlier friendly exchange they'd enjoyed. "Other than the Rutledges, you mean?" he asked, one eyebrow raised in disdain. "You can see there is a great wrong there, when a lady like Diana Atwood can be abused like this and no one does anything."

"Yes, that I can see," she said. She pushed at the heavy curls that were falling down from her elaborate coiffure. "I was merely trying to make pleasant conversation, milord." She stressed his title.

"I asked you not to milord me. I see you are the same old stubborn, controlling miss you ever were."

Color rushed to her cheeks. "I beg your pardon!"

"And well you might. Your friend—at least I believed you to be friends—lies wounded in there and you try to make light conversation. You remind me of the silly young misses flocking to Almack's to snag a mate. Revolting."

"And I see you're the same...!" Anna caught her lip between her teeth. She must not fight with this irritating man while Diana was in need of cool heads. "Really, we mustn't fight. You have Diana's best interests at heart, as do I. Can we not put down our cudgels and be friends?"

He glared at her, his black eyes boring into her. "Certainly. Nothing could make me happier." He turned away and began to pace in the small room.

Anna Kate sighed, then sat down on a small, upholstered chair.

His head whipped around and he again stared at her. "And just what are you sighing over, miss?"

"I apologize again," she said. "It's merely that you remind me of a bull in a china shop, the way you fling yourself about. Can't you find a place to sit? You are nerve-making, with your undisciplined pacings."

He stopped his pacing, stuck his fists on his hips and began to speak. Then he bit off the tirade he had obviously planned to loose on her. She wondered what he'd stopped himself from saying.

Quill straightened, dropping his hands to his

side. He looked like a soldier snapping to attention. He spoke at last. "I am taking my leave, Miss Forsythe. Please give Diana my regards when you can speak to her. And tell her I'll be back."

With that he spun on his heels and stomped out of the room. She heard the front door slam.

Mme Veronique entered the sewing room. "O la la, that man is in a taking. What did you say to him?"

Even though Mme Vero did not sound as though she was scolding her, Anna burst into tears. "I don't know! It seems everything I say makes him angry! I was trying to make light conversation during this difficult time of waiting to find out from the doctor—oh! Has he said? How is Diana doing?" She took the lace handkerchief Mme Vero handed her. "Thank you. I think that's why Quill was angry with me."

Mme Vero shook her head in confusion. "Why?"

"Because I am too self-absorbed. Everything I turn to me, even my friend's dire situation. Oh, what shall I do?"

"*Je suppose*," the Frenchwoman began, "I suppose you can wait fifteen years to be middle-aged, but Milord the Earl of Wentworth may not wait that long. You are merely young. It will pass, *crois-moi, ma petite*." She smiled at Anna and patted her cheek. "Your friend will *probablement* survive, with good care. I told *M. le docteur* you will see to that, *n'est-ce pas?*"

Anna sniffed. "Oh, yes, I will. Thank you, Madame. I appreciate your kindness to us today. Can she leave?"

The doctor poked his shaggy head into the sewing room. "She will have to leave, young woman. Where is your common sense? You think a milliner's shop is the place for a seriously ill person to recuperate?" He gestured with his head back into the front room of the shop. Both Anna and Mme Vero followed him. Diana was sleeping on a low fainting couch at the side of the room. "You go get someone to pick her up in a horse-drawn conveyance, the plusher the better. She needs the gentlest of handling."

By now Anna Kate's tears had returned and were pouring down her face.

"Stop that crying," Mr. Sumner barked. "You'd think you were the patient."

She sniffed. "Yes, sir. You are right. As Madame was just telling me, I am self-absorbed and childish."

"That is not what I said," Mme Vero remonstrated.

"Close enough." She straightened up, took a deep breath, and tugged at the waist of her dress to signify she was ready for whatever they wanted to tell her. She would no longer be childish, but mature and responsible. "I'll go get my aunt Stanfield's carriage. Tell my friend if she awakens that I will return."

Feeling torn, she cast a wistful glance at the recumbent form. Her hand on the knob, she began to open the door when it burst inward, surprising her. It was Quill. She nearly gasped when she saw his face and those burning eyes. "Oh! It's you!"

She lowered her eyes and bit her lip. Would he hear the pleased surprise in her voice? Would he know how much he affected her?

He had no respect for her, that was sure; her heart constricted at the thought.

She felt a blush rise up her neck and into her face. She wanted to stamp her feet and scream! She could not at this point let him see—! "I...," she stuttered, "I need to go order a carriage for Diana. She can be moved..."

Before she could complete her sentence, he spoke. "I've brought my landau. It may not be the best means of moving her, but it will have to do." His voice was cold, business-like, cutting her heart to the core.

He did not even like her! He had when they were children. She knew he had.

Even then, however, they had clashed. He was single-minded and pursued whatever goal he aimed for without swerving. He had accused her of being a flibbertigibbet, never settling on any goal. He had been wrong, though.

But she couldn't change his attitude about her, that she knew. At least not today.

Death in Exile

Quill Rossiter glared at Anna Kate Forsythe standing before him. *In faith she is an irritating miss!* he thought. He was glad she had rejected him three years ago: if she hadn't and he had become romantically involved with her, he'd never succeed at getting the law of the land changed in respect to treatment of prisoners.

That bit of teasing earlier about Brutus and the animals she had smuggled indoors when they were children: it nearly made him lower his guard against a pretty face. Then, when she later played the coquette, he had wanted to grab her and kiss her. It was proper that he'd become harsh to regain his purpose. Sometimes he fell too easily into lightheartedness. He couldn't, not now, if he was to accomplish his goal.

He knew he was defying convention when he became so heated about issues of injustice. It took much self-control to overcome strong emotions on the topic of criminal reform.

He now more closely examined her face. She looked close to tears. He felt sure his earlier brusqueness had brought her to this pass. He couldn't apologize for it, however. The social graces were artificial and worthless when reform in government was needed. Only passion for justice, pursued with blinders on, would achieve the changes justice demanded.

Schunk

She turned her head away, he was sure, to keep from looking at him. Yes, it was best if she disliked him. What if he began to pursue her, what if he fell in love with her all over again? He had decided months ago that he must remain unmarried. He could not marry if he was to stay single-minded in his crusade to end the cruelty of the British prison system.

Now Mr. Sumner brought him back to the present. "Well, where're your men? Don't just stand there like a lump. Get her moved," he barked.

Anna Kate jumped, and Quill fought the urge to salute the domineering little doctor. Instead, he merely said, "Yes, sir."

Anna Kate pushed past Quill and dashed from the milliner's shop. She must get home before she began to cry again. Why did Quill Rossiter have the power to upset her so?

As she walked quickly back to the Stanfields, she thought about him. "At least I likely will never have to face him again." When her heart plummeted at the thought, she felt her mind and heart warring with each other. Which did she prefer: to have to deal with him all day every day, or never again? *I do not know, I just do not know.*

Then the thought of Diana struck her. *If he keeps Diana at his house, will I be able to see her? I must keep tabs on how she is doing!*

Once she'd reached the Stanfields' house, a new thought stopped her in her tracks. The events of the morning told her one important fact. "It is Diana he loves," she whispered. "I know it. Why did I not see it before?" Her tears began to flow again. She bit her lower lip to stop them, but it didn't work this time. She couldn't blame him. Diana had always been beautiful as well as kind and gracious, never the hoyden Anna herself had been.

Diana deserved Quill; Anna didn't. But how would Diana get out of her disastrous marriage, alive, at least?

Anna entered the house quietly and climbed the stairs to her third-floor room across from Mary and Paul's nursery. She slipped into her room with gratitude. She hoped to escape their curious eyes until she had removed her cloak and gloves and repaired the ravages her tears had wreaked on her face. How could she answer their questions? She could not express even to herself why she was so emotional.

And to hide the pouch Diana had given into her keeping. Where—she looked around the room before settling on the large walnut wardrobe. She stuffed her reticule, the pouch inside, in a box in the back of the wardrobe, with her other reticules.

The room was warm and inviting, though simply furnished. Constance Stanfield, Aunt Lydia's daughter-in-law, had had the room freshly done in a soft blue for Anna's arrival months before, in May. The angel tester above the bed was pale blue gauze, like a summer sky. An old blue and cream Oriental rug warmed the hardwood floor, and a blue and white ewer and washbowl stood on a cherrywood stand to the left of the door. She appreciated the simple graciousness of Constance's efforts to make her comfortable.

She hurried to the washstand to dash cool water on her face. A large mirror hung above the stand. She looked at her reflection in the wavy glass, then stuck her tongue out at it. She was not pleased with her face this day!

At that moment she heard a light tap at the door. "Oh, no!" she said softly. "Not now."

She patted her face dry, smoothed her windblown hair, and then tugged at her dress to stall a moment. Then she walked slowly, as if to the gallows, to open it.

At the door stood Constance Stanfield. Concern lined her face. "Are you all right, Anna Kate? You came in so quietly and then didn't speak when you passed me in the lower hall."

"Oh, I am sorry! What will you think of my manners?" She opened the door wide to invite Constance in. She tried to smile at the beautiful woman before her. Glossy dark brown hair, wide brown eyes, and a rosebud mouth set in a heart-shaped face—Constance's looks made Anna feel dowdy. Constance was invariably sweet to Anna, showing her gratitude for her help now while Ansten, Anna's cousin, was in Canada. And they were friends, allies against Aunt Lydia's efforts to take over everything in the household. They frequently laughed over Ansten's comment, "Mother would make a better general than Wellington, or Boney either."

Constance took both of Anna's hands in hers. "What is the matter, Anna Kate? I don't want to intrude, but may I help?"

The deep, sincere compassion that radiated from the beautiful woman set Anna Kate to crying again. Constance put an arm around her shoulders and led her to a small sofa covered with powder blue satin. "Here, use my handkerchief. You never seem to have your own, dear one."

The gentle teasing made Anna laugh. "I have made such a cake of myself. I just met two old friends from childhood, a happy event that has devastated me!" She went on to tell Constance of the morning meetings with Diana and Quill. She did not give Diana's name or too many details, for without thinking Constance could let Diana's whereabouts slip to the wrong people. "The worst part of it all is that my friend is in terrible straits, yet I feel sorry for myself because Quill does not love me! Such a silly goose I am."

She straightened her back and blinked to clear the tears. "I am fine now, truly I am. Thank you for listening to me catastrophize."

Constance squeezed her shoulders, then kissed

her forehead. "It is my pleasure, Anna Kate. You're such a sunbeam in our household."

Anna smiled at her. "You will never know how much your words mean. My heart is so sore from Quill's harsh words. Thank you." She stood. "Where are Mary and Paul? Has Aunt Lydia returned from the museum with them?"

"Not yet. They're due soon. Wash up and come join us for lunch. Then they can return to their lessons with you."

Anna Kate smiled again. "I will. Thank you." She would be glad to go back to the children's lessons once more. She had developed a small coterie of young women back in Andover who had come to her for lessons in Latin, music, and the classics. Quill may dislike her, but she was a good teacher, an excellent one, even.

Briefly she wondered if she should return home before her Christmas leave. That way she could avoid meeting him again.

But did she want to avoid him? She knew, in spite of his treatment of her, that she did not.

CHAPTER 3

Quill gestured to two men outside Mme Vero's door. His footman and coachman entered, tugging at their forelocks as they acknowledged Mme Vero's presence. "I brought some help."

"Not enough!" Mr. Sumner said. "You young people have no sense. Have to help you myself." He trundled over to the couch where Diana lay. He put one beefy hand on her shoulder. "Miss, Miss?"

Quill was surprised to see how gentle the man was with her.

Diana opened her eyes.

The doctor smiled gently down on her. "Some men are here to move you, dear. I will be sure that they are careful, that they do not hurt you."

"Thank you," she whispered.

Quill was grateful to be on the street once again. He was in the open air, where he could breathe.

It was too maddening to be in the company of Anna Kate Forsythe for more than five minutes! Yet, he was relieved to have the sorrowful responsibility of moving Diana Atwood—Rutledge, that is, he corrected himself—to his house in Mayfair.

When his carriage turned into Park Lane, he saw a curricle with a matched set of bays standing at his door. He recognized it as belonging to Toby Esterby. An old drinking and gambling chum, Toby had been in Belgium with Wellington, then posted to Canada. Quill would normally be pleased to see him, safely back from war, but today?

Toby had apparently just arrived, for he was halfway up the steep run of fifteen marble steps leading to the imposing oak doors of the Georgian house. When he heard Quill's coach, he turned and ran down the steps two at a time. The sight of the gangly man, all elbows and knees, made Quill smile. This morning Toby's long red hair flopped up and down over his high forehead. He looked a scarecrow, with his long skinny limbs flying in his baggy clothing. Even his stockings looked baggy.

Quill laughed, and Coachman John looked at him in surprise.

"Oh, I know, man," Quill said. "Even though

I'm deep in worry over Diana, I can't help but laugh at Toby."

When Quill stepped from his carriage, Toby grinned and saluted him. "It's back from the wars I am! Ain't you pleased to see me? Your face looks long enough to step on."

Quill grabbed his friend's arm, then pumped his hand hard twice. "Man, you know it's good to see you. I am on an errand of mercy, however, so my face reflects that, no doubt."

Toby's gaze followed where Quill pointed, to the pale woman lying against the leathern squabs of the seat. "Well, see here, that's Diana from home! And she don't look too good."

"Help me move her, quickly, and I'll tell you the story." He now spoke to Diana who had opened her eyes. "We are at my town house. We will do our best to be careful, Diana, darling. And if it please you, I will tell Toby the sad tale."

She started. "But what if he tells..."

"Toby has no love for Henry Rutledge. You're safe with him."

"Henry Rutledge? The Beast? He's brought you to this pass? 'Pon my word, you're safe with us, milady."

She smiled weakly at the earnest young man. "Yes, Lord Wentworth, you may share my secret with Sir Toby."

Once the four men—Toby, Quill, and his two menservants—had moved Diana into Quill's library on the first floor, Quill rang for the housekeeper.

"Mrs. Godwin," he said, "I have a house guest, but you do not know that. You have not seen any young woman here today or any day or night recently. Isn't that correct?"

The short, round-faced woman nodded her head firmly. Her eyes wide, she said, "Yes, milord, not today or any day. Or night." She looked now at Diana. The kindness written on her face with its soft wrinkles told Quill, and Diana too, that they would have no worries at her hand.

"I know I don't have to say that goes for you two also, John and Collins." They both nodded. He could trust every member of his household with his very life.

He gave brief instructions to the two men on how to carry her up to the guestroom. "Use this chair," he said, pointing to a light lady's chair by his mother's desk, "and handle her gently."

Once Mrs. Godwin, Coachman John, and Collins were gone with their precious burden, Quill began to tell Toby what he knew of the latest beating Diana had suffered at Rutledge's hand. "It's frustrating not to be able to stop him. But he always chooses a time when no one sees, when I am gone from London or some such thing. And he probably murdered Mathers—do you remember her, Diana's family housekeeper?"

"I' faith, he's a mean 'un," Toby said. "What're you goin' to do about this, Quill?"

Death in Exile

"Obviously the first thing to do is to hide Diana and get her well." At this point he began to tell Toby of Anna's aid to Diana that morning. "She is so maddening, Toby."

"You did always say that. I say, my man, which of the two lovely damsels are you in love with? You sound so protective and fond when you speak to Diana, yet the passion Anna Kate arouses in you means to me that you're wild about her."

"Wild about that little lightbrain? You must be joking!" Quill began pacing around the well-appointed room. His mother had decorated it for him the year before, in navy and maroon. It was a handsome room.

"Whoa! Don't throttle me! You always did respond strongly to 'that little lightbrain.' I dare, in spite of feeling in danger for my life, speak the truth. You're passionately in love with Anna Kate. Is she as lovely now as her youthful beauty promised those years ago?"

"Lovelier!" Quill flushed. "See how she befuddles me? She turned me down three years ago, Toby. And besides, she is not the appropriate helpmeet for my campaign. I would spend all my time sparring with her or fixing the messes she gets herself into." After a brief pause, he turned and stared at Toby. "You can tell I'm in love with her? What must she think?" He paced some more. "No," he said, more to himself than to Toby, "I made sure she believed I had no interest in her. You would

never credit how rude I was to her." He smiled ruefully. "But back to Diana and her situation."

"Sure," Toby said, peering at his friend out of a
corner of his eye. "You were telling me what you
plan to do about Rutledge."

"Right. The first thing is to keep Diana safe.
The second is to stop Rutledge in whatever his
scheme is. We have known from the first that he
married Diana for her money. Now he has gone
through much of it with his gambling and woman-
izing, in the Prince Regent's company, so he ex-
pects no consequences of his behavior. He wants
the portion she inherited from her mother's side,
but she will not sign it over. He means to force her
to or to put her away so he can get it."

"Heinous, my man, quite heinous. But I don't
see how you'll bring him to book."

Quill sighed. He crossed the room to the fireplace, where he leaned against the mantel, head on
his hands, a picture of defeat. "I don't know either."

He began to talk about his dreams for his ten-
ure in the House of Lords. "You know Wilberforce
has been railing against slavery for all these years.
He did get the slave trade abolished, but still he tries
and tries to emancipate those still enslaved. I have
to fight the transportation of convicts, just as he
has fought the slave trade."

He turned a tormented face to his friend, who
was still sitting across the room. "The treatment of
convicts in those hellish ships is every bit as cruel

and unconscionable as it was in the slavers." He pounded the mantel with one fist. "It must end."

Toby shook his head. "I don't know, Quill..."

"Toby, this is of prime consequence."

"Yes, man, I know your feelings, but these criminals must be stopped. You can hardly walk the streets these days without bein' accosted..."

"By *Diana*?" Scorn dripped from his voice. "Don't you see? Not all the accused are guilty. There must be others like Diana who are falsely accused."

He slammed a fist into his left hand. "I know those who break the law need to be punished, but does the punishment have to be the inhumane and cruel treatment they are at present subjected to? How can treating people like beasts, even worse than you or I would treat our dogs or horses, teach them to behave? The current mood of the country—ever more and ever harsher punishments—does not, cannot end the stealing and the robbing done to provide the bare essentials of life to these poor wretches! God in Heaven must detest us all, those who mistreat the wretches and those of us who allow it!"

Toby's mouth had dropped open during this speech. "You are truly frightening when you get so impassioned. You'll make children run screaming to their mamas when you deliver that 'un. Can't you lighten up?"

Quill spread his hands in supplication. "But can't you see—this is of such great import! I cannot remain the cool patrician Society would like me to be. I cannot. I think of Mother's friend Jane Austen and her dislike of 'enthusiasm,' but I cannot strangle it." His shoulders drooped. "Can you, even you, not understand?"

Toby smiled at him. "I'll try, my man. I do believe I've just heard the best speech ever, even in the Lords. I must stand and applaud." He stood, then his lovably homely face sobered. "You have a long haul ahead of you. Everyone is yelling that crime has risen since Waterloo. I think it's because of all those poor buggers out of work and no war to go fight in."

Quill nodded. "I don't doubt it. That's why I feel I have to do something. I beg your most fervent support, Toby."

Toby stuck out his hand, which Quill grabbed like a life line. "You have it, man. You have it."

CHAPTER 4

Henry Rutledge waited for his man to return to the Two Swans. His fury rose as he paced in the private room he'd rented off the main pub. A hamhock fist slammed into an open palm. He would hurt someone if that woman wasn't found soon.

His beefy neck held up a large, square head. Thin brown hair barely covered his scalp. He wasn't ashamed of his broad shoulders or powerful hips and legs. He was an oak tree, and that weeping willow of a wife wasn't going to beat him out of his rights.

He heard a commotion in the larger room. Stepping through the doorway, he saw that lady's purse Lucas Cranford enter. Maybe Cranford knew where Diana was. He'd certainly been moonsick over her for years. Rutledge laughed. He, Henry Rutledge, had ended up with the prize though, not the pretty young baron. Thinking furiously, he planned what he might say to the man, in order to extract any information he might have.

Gesturing to a barmaid, Henry stood in the shadow of the wide doorframe. "Say, see that man who just entered?"

"The bonny man with the fair hair?" She was close to salivating over Cranford, dressed as he was in royal blue and daffodil. "Quite a popinjay, ain't he?"

"That one. Ask him to come speak to me." He placed a coin in her hand.

The ready smile on Lucas Cranford's face faded when he saw Henry Rutledge. "What do you want?" he asked, his voice frosty.

"Always a poor sport, aren't you, Cranford? I was in town with my lady wife and wondered if you would like to visit with her, pass the time of day. I have no hard feelings toward you." He smiled, his face tight.

"Why should you? You ended up with the prize." Cranford's left eye began to twitch, a sure sign he was feeling unsure of himself. Handsome he may be, a poker face never.

"Would you like to see her?" Rutledge continued. He felt sweat spring up at the back of his neck. He couldn't tell from the other man's demeanor whether he knew where Diana was. "Today?"

Cranford's eyes shifted, and he licked his lips. "Surely. Where is she?"

"Shopping, of a certainty. You know women, once in London, always in the shops. Come by for tea, at say five."

"Where?"

"My townhouse, of course. Stafford Hall, in Mayfair."

"Diana's townhouse, don't you mean."

Rutledge grinned, sure of a winning hand. "Mine now," he said softly. He looked up when he detected a rustle at the door. His man had returned. He dismissed Cranford with a curt nod, then shook his head a bit to Walters.

"Well?" he barked at his man once Lucas was out of earshot.

Walters looked around, then whispered to Rutledge. "Neither hide nor hair, sir. Not a trace."

Rutledge clenched his fist and drove it into the heavy plastered wall beside him. "See that man? He's dressed bright enough anyone can follow him in the deepest gloom. Go hire that detective in Fleet Street the Prince recommended. Tell him to stick to Cranford, see if he leads the detective to her."

"Sir," Walters said, then tugged his forelock and backed out of the dimly lit room.

The Beast smiled, then sat down at the small round table by the fireplace. He reached for the bottle of claret and poured himself a glass. He'd be on to her at last.

Lucas Cranford, baron of Breckin, spoke briefly to

his friends in the pub. "I am leaving. An important appointment slipped my mind." He stepped carefully out of the Two Swans, reining in his fury. He did not want Rutledge or anyone else to guess just how impotent he felt.

He paused outside the inn. He needed to compose himself before facing even the liveryman when he reclaimed his horse. He tugged at his lower lip with a thumb and forefinger.

Diana was supposed to have married him, not that ox Rutledge. Why was Rutledge behaving so magnanimously? It didn't suit his uncouth, encroaching ways.

Cranford had heard all the gossip about Rutledge's gambling and whoring in the Prince Regent's company. He'd heard Henry was burning chasms in Diana's wealth. He clenched his teeth. Rutledge wanted something from him. What was it?

Anna Kate heard the nursery door open, then close. Aunt Lydia and the children were back. She was glad—this day had passed so slowly, once she had told Constance her tale of Diana and Quillen.

She rose from the desk where she had been writing her father a long letter, one that struck even her as artificial, since she could not tell him the thing that mattered, about running into Diana. She sighed.

Death in Exile

What a quandary to be in!

In her letter she had briefly spoken of seeing Quill. She did not mention how he had upset her, with his looks, his appeal to her of old, or his rudeness. Papa would never understand.

Her door burst open before she reached it. Mary and Paul rushed in, throwing themselves at her waist. "Oh, come, Anna Kate, and see what Grandfather sent us!"

She looked up at Aunt Lydia, who said in explanation, "Constance's father." Lydia had been widowed for many years.

To the children Anna said, "A new bauble?"

"Bigger than a bauble!" Paul said. "A pony."

"And a cart, with fringe on the canopy," Mary said. "And he said I get to drive it too, once we get teached."

"Taught," Anna Kate corrected absently. "Let me see this splendid beast. I imagine he is quite stunning."

"She," Mary said, "and she is lovely."

Paul rolled his eyes. At eight he thought lovely mares were not as dashing as stallions. "When I am older, he has promised me a black stallion."

"Then you would like Lord Wentworth's stallion. He is black," Anna told him. "Perhaps he will bring the horse by soon. Brutus is the horse's name, and he behaves like a trained dog."

Paul's eyes grew large. "Really?"

"Yes, really. I'll send a note to ask him to come

visit." She chided herself: was this visit for her or for the child?

Mary grasped her hand. "Come! No more talky talky. Come see our pony."

Constance joined the children and smiled over their heads at Anna. "Children, do not prattle on. Give Miss Anna room to breathe!"

"Yes, Mama," they both replied obediently. But Mary gave one last tug at her beloved Anna's hand.

All four of them made their way down the wide, curving front stairs. Some of Anna's joy of the morning returned to her, now that she had the children to occupy her mind. Perhaps she could forget having seen Quill today—but she could not forget Diana! She must go see her friend. And she would be sure not to go with a Friday face. She must smile and be gracious, even if Quillen Rossiter, fourth earl of Wentworth, tasked her for it. He had been rude and despicable, and his behavior would not influence hers, of that she would be sure.

The two children grabbed her hands to pull her out the front door where the cart and horse were waiting. Constance laughed. "I will ask that lunch be held for ten minutes. But only ten minutes, children."

"Yes, Mama," they both replied.

The dappled gray pony and blue and white cart were quite lovely. "I see why you love your horse, Mary dear," Anna said to the small girl. Mary, who even at four had her mother's dark brown hair and rosy skin, smiled sweetly.

Paul offered the pony a carrot. When the small mare had eaten it, she began to search in Paul's jacket pocket for more food. Not finding any, she nudged him hard, nearly knocking him down.

"Paul," Anna said to the handsome boy with his father's black hair and green eyes, "I do believe she will need a firm hand. It is good you are so strong." That gratified the boy, whose chest swelled a bit with pride.

"Let's take a ride, now," he said masterfully.

"Yes," Mary seconded, preparing to climb into the cart, "now."

"Not now, dear. Your mama is waiting lunch." Anna took Mary by the hand and gently led her charges back toward the house.

At lunch Aunt Lydia asked Anna Kate to come to her sitting room later. An unaccustomed scowl sat on the older woman's face. "Something I have failed to do with you has been brought to my mind." When Anna Kate asked what it was, she shook her head. "I will talk to you in fifteen minutes, not before."

Her brusque tone surprised Anna. While walking the children back to the nursery for their afternoon rest, she tried to understand the situation.

Her aunt was rarely cross with her, or anyone

41

else. In truth, Aunt Lydia was usually too preoccupied to be cross. She believed, now that the children's father was gone to war, that she had the responsibility to oversee their education. All her spare time went to their training.

Anna pondered. Had she done something wrong? She decided it must have to do with the earlier fiasco with Quill. Perhaps Mme Veronique had told Aunt Lydia that Anna Kate had not behaved well with him. But no—Vero had not seemed critical of her, only indulgent.

She was developing a headache. She wasn't used to thinking so furiously.

Mary began to cry once they reached the nursery, disappointed that they were not going out for a ride in the cart. "But you promised, Miss Anna."

Anna examined her face. Her eyes looked dull and heavy. Her natural rosy cheeks looked beet red. Anna placed the inside of her wrist against Mary's cheeks. "Oh, dear. I fear you may be feverish."

Mary's face fell. "Oh, no," she wailed, "now you won't let me out again for a ride!"

Paul grimaced at his little sister. "Don't play the baby, Mary. We will never get to ride if you fuss."

"You need to rest first, my pet," Anna said firmly. "You must be overtired, you see, to cry so easily. If you feel better, we'll go later, before tea. And I'll ask a footman to take a note to Lord Wentworth. Perhaps he will introduce you to his stallion."

The thought comforted Mary. Paul it seemed to thrill, for his eyes gleamed. "That would be smashing."

Anna Kate handed them over to the care of Betsy, the nursery maid. She kissed Mary on the forehead. "I will return after your rest time, little one."

Leaving them with Martha, the nursery maid, she sighed. Her headache was worsening. What a day! Diana injured, Quillen angry, and now Mary sickening. And Aunt Lydia so serious with her. What was the problem there?

She sighed again. *I must see what Aunt Lydia wants first. I can only hope it is a problem easily solved.*

The way things had been going all morning, however, she doubted that would be the case.

She descended from the nursery floor to the first floor where Aunt Lydia had her suite of rooms in the back. She stepped quietly through the hall, not wanting to disturb Constance if she were trying to rest in the front suite.

Anna knocked softly on her aunt's door.

"Come in!"

She entered to find the older woman sitting at her *secretaire* writing a letter. She watched as Aunt Lydia signed her name with her usual flourish and then dusted sand across the ink to set it. She then tipped the sheet of paper over the crystal jar of sand and blew gently, to get the excess off the heavy vellum. "That is done."

Aunt Lydia rose from her chair, then crossed the room to where Anna was awaiting her wishes. Placing a hand on Anna's elbow, she led the young woman across to a divan covered in primrose damask. Once she had seated herself and Anna, she shook her head. "My dear, it has come to my attention that I have failed you grievously."

Her gravity increased Anna Kate's alarm. "What...what do you mean, Aunt?"

"I have a note from Lord Wentworth's mother. She is an old friend of mine, you know. She is down from Andover and heard I had not yet gotten you an invitation to Almack's."

Still her face was filled with sobriety.

Anna nearly burst out laughing. "Oh, dear Aunt Lydia, is that all?"

Aunt Lydia bristled, then echoed her niece's words. "'Is that all?' I am quite derelict in my duty. What would your dear mother—and worse, your grandmother!—say? Your family, on Sarah's and my side, ranks with any of the *ton*. You are entitled to be introduced to Society. Your father, dear as he is, is somewhat narrow, and even absent-minded. He sent you here for the serious matter of learning to earn your living, forgetting you can associate with the *ton*. But as Lady Wentworth pointed out, you do not need to earn your living, not with the blood of the Windesors in your veins!" She turned her head away and covered her lips with a finger. Then she tapped her lips. "Whatever was I thinking of? You cannot work as a governess here."

"Oh, but Aunt Lydia, you can't send me off! The children and Constance—they rely on me. And I love the children. I promised to stay until Christmas at least. You cannot send me off."

"Hush. Let me think. You may stay here of course—you must! I will begin dressing you for the season, you can continue to keep the children company, and I will talk to Lord Wentworth about getting a voucher to Almack's. The Season is upon us."

Anna gasped. "Oh, my goodness, Lord Wentworth."

"What about him?"

She held one hand up to her splitting head. "He will hate me. He thought I was too giddy for words this morning when I tried to be gracious and converse lightly. He was so serious and grim. He will surely despise me if he thinks I'm wangling a voucher to Almack's. Please do not ask him. Anyone else but him. Please, dear Aunt!"

"Don't be a goose. Of course I must ask him. The time is slipping away from me. What will his mother say if I fail to get you ready straight away? If only Ansten were here, he could handle all this for us."

The short, round-faced woman stood and began pacing in the wide, spacious room, done in cerulean and several shades of yellow with touches of primrose. It was a cheery room, but today she didn't seem to notice. Wringing her hands she said, "How could I have failed to realize...?" She threw her hands down at her side and straightened. "Well. No time for foolishness. You are excused, dear. I have written your father to inform him of my error. Blessedly, I know he will not task me for it. He is such a lamb. Next, I must write Lord Wentworth." She returned to her desk where she sat down and took out another sheet of vellum. In the next second she turned back to Anna, mouth gaping, eyes wide. "Oh, no! I let you go to the shops alone this morning!"

A cold *frisson* coursed through Anna's veins. Her small freedoms would surely end if Aunt Lydia carried through this new passion. No walks by herself, no trips to the shops. Well-born young ladies were virtual prisoners of society, while their elders shopped for matches in marriage for them! How could she deter Aunt Lydia from this course?

Perhaps she could not, but then again, perhaps she could gain a small reprieve.

Anna rose from the divan and crossed to her aunt's side. "Dear Aunt Lydia," she stated quietly, "Papa will not task you nor will I. But please, wait at least three days before you write Lord Wentworth. I promised the children..."

Her aunt startled, as though unaware Anna was still in the room with her. "Oh, are you still there? You are excused."

"No, please hear me. Please wait to write him

for three days."

"Three days! Of course not. No time, no time." She shook her head and half a dozen hairpins flew out of her hair.

"I must write him a note to ask him to bring his horse to show the children the stallion's tricks. I promised them, Aunt Lydia."

It seemed her aunt's eyes focused, and at last she heard Anna's words. "Oh, a promise, eh?"

"Yes, ma'am. Please would you hold off? I'm afraid—well, I'm afraid he'll refuse to show them the horse if he decides I'm just trying to get him to get me into Almacks." She hoped that would be a sufficient reason to convince her aunt: she did not want to explain about Diana, nor about the fact that she wanted to see Quill when he came, if he came.

Quillen had plenty on his mind at the moment as it was. He would perhaps disdain her request to indulge the children. But perhaps he would not. She remembered a kindly younger Quill who never failed to perform a favor if asked.

"Well."

Anna watched as Aunt Lydia's mind seemed to rearrange itself to the new plan.

"Three days?"

"Merely three days."

"Agreed," she said firmly, "but only three, you understand."

"Yes, ma'am. And thank you." With those words Anna Kate threw herself into her roly-poly aunt's arms and hugged her. "I will be as docile as a kitten for any of your future plans." To herself she added, *Or at least I'll try.*

Chapter 5

Early Monday morning Quillen Rossiter joined his mother in the large mahogany paneled dining room. She had arrived from Moondown Manor, their estate in Andover, only the night before. They made a practice of meeting over breakfast, whether in London or back in Andover. "It is good to see you, Mother." He leaned over to kiss her cheek. "You are looking lovely as ever."

She wore a lilac morning gown, which set off the soft silver of her hair and the pale violet of her eyes. She had been a beautiful woman and had good bones still. He noted with some concern a slight grayish tinge to her skin.

"You are up early today," she said, a smile for her well-loved son lighting her face.

"Yes, I must have the doctor in again for Diana. Mother, she is not doing well."

She nodded, concern etching lines on her face. "I know, her fever is up again. I will order another bath for her."

Just then Randall, the butler, entered with a letter for Quill. He handed it over silently. He was used to Wentworth's sullen sulks, so he expected no reply.

Quill opened the seal, then the vellum page. He scowled. "It's from Anna Kate Forsythe," he said crossly.

Eleanor Rossiter, Lady Wentworth, raised her head. "You make her sound like a dunning agent. You two were such sweet playmates when you were young."

"When I saw her last week while searching for Diana, she acted silly and dithery, precisely when her concern for Diana ought to have made her sober!"

"I vow," she said lightly, "your black visage frightened her so, she did not even know her name."

He ignored her comment. "And now a note from her asking after Diana's health, but also a request that I ride Brutus over to amuse the children she is nursemaiding."

"Terrible!" she said, teasing in earnest. "That is a dreadful thing to do."

He grinned at her. "I take your point. But my dear lady Mother, she seems so young."

"She is. There are worse things to be, I would say." Eleanor changed her tone to become serious. "It came to my attention back in Andover that Anna Kate is working. I was very concerned."

"Why? Best thing for a silly goose like her!"

"Quillen, listen. She is a descendant of Guy Windesor on her mother's side. You know her as the daughter of a humble village vicar. But she is more."

Quill glared at her. "None of this seems very important at the moment, Mother. Not with Diana..." He gestured abovestairs.

"Oh, but it is! She should have a Season so that she has a chance at the marriage mart, Quillen. I had so hoped..."

"What did you hope?"

"Oh, some years ago, three or four, that you were going to ask for her hand."

"So did I. But she refused me."

"Refused you! When?"

"Just before I left Andover three years ago. It was Boxing Day, I recall, and I had delivered presents to her house from you and Father."

"How did it happen?"

"She was in the music room at the vicarage, looking, well, adorable, as she could, you know. I began to ask her, but she said, 'Not now, Quill.'"

"How did you begin to ask? I cannot believe—!"

"She was sitting at the piano, playing something by Bach, I believe, and I leaned over to whisper in her ear. And she said, 'Not now.'"

"And what did you do?"

"What else should I do? I grabbed my cloak and

left. Her father walked in right then, and I did take my leave of him quite courteously, but then I left."

"I wonder whether you misunderstood. Or she misunderstood you? This does not ring true."

"It is true, Mother. Would I lie to you? She is too young for me anyway."

Eleanor sighed. "Yes, dear. But I wish you would ask her again."

"Never! If she were the last female in the world, I would not ask her again."

Eleanor lay one palm up to ask for his hand in hers. When he gave it to her, she rubbed her thumb over the back of his hand. "But now she needs to find another man to marry, then. She has the right to a Season. Although I understand from Lydia Stanfield she does not want it."

He shifted in his chair and propped up his chin on his right hand. "Oh? Somehow that redeems her, in my eyes."

She frowned at her son. "You do realize what future lies ahead of her if she does not marry well, impoverished gentility, or just plain poverty."

He shrugged. It didn't seem crucial to him. "Or she could marry a rotter like Henry Rutledge and be lying near her death, all her beauty and charm of no value to her."

"I am here to give your household propriety while Diana is here, but also to help Lydia launch Anna Kate. I consider it my duty too, seeing as how she is from home. You will help us?"

Death in Exile

He stood abruptly, nearly knocking his chair down in his haste. "I do not like to refuse you anything, dear Mother, but in this I will not help you. It is frivolous and ridiculous, in the extreme." He turned on his heel, then back again. "Okay, maybe I will, but just for you. I'll send a note acquiescing in her request. Also, I'll send for the doctor. Diana needs to be seen to. Then I will ride over to the Stanfields to show off my trick horse to some children." With that he stomped out of the room.

Eleanor sighed. He was such an intense man. He wore even her out with the strength of his passions. She pressed a hand against her heart. He would make it difficult for her to help bring Anna Kate out if he learned of her new heart problem. She would tell him later, but not now. She rose from her chair and made her way out of the large dining room. She needed to see to Diana.

Quill swung easily up onto the large black stallion when the groom had finished saddling him. Turning the magnificent horse out of the mews, he breathed deeply. The air was sharp and clear. He could smell charcoal still smoking in the chestnut sellers' braziers from the night before.

Schunk

Quill was thankful few others were up yet to clog the narrow streets. He noticed a few late roses blooming in the park at the end of his street.

His mind flowed freely, switching back and forth between Diana and Anna Kate. Each so different, almost like different kingdoms of values. Then he thought of his mother. In his mind's eye an image formed of her as a bridge between the two kingdoms.

He shook his head to clear it of his fancies. In spite of outward differences, he knew, from their essential childhood selves, that Diana and Anna did not differ much. Only their present circumstances set off their differences now.

His mother had been right. He was unfairly judging Anna now, merely because she seemed to be in more favorable circumstances than Diana was. And yet his mother had pointed out, perhaps rightly, that Anna Kate's situation was potentially dire also.

The marriage mart. It all came down to that, the English notion of propriety and the marriage mart.

Women were viewed as property, even if rather precious, valuable property. If they lost their beauty or refused to worship at their husbands' or guardians' feet, or if once married they did not bear male progeny, they rapidly lost value. It was not fair. He felt his heart constrict. It was not just.

Quill's heart lifted when he saw the Stanfields'

mansion rise before him. It was quite trim and neat, with well-polished brasses on the door and manicured yews along the wide, curving steps up to the house. The house reminded him he now had a chance to make amends for his earlier boorishness.

He resolved to treat Anna better than he had several days earlier. Blame was not to be laid at her feet for being young or foolish. How could he expect her to see the wider world as he did?

And perhaps he should reconsider his refusal to help his mother's attempts to marry the girl off. It was the least he could do.

Tying Brutus to the stanchion in front, he walked briskly up to the door. A rotund butler opened the door to him.

"I am here to see Miss Forsythe and the children. I believe they are interested in horseflesh these days," he said with a smile, his good spirits high with his new resolve.

"Yes, milord. Your note just arrived, and she is expecting you. This way please." He waved Quill into the drawing room. "May I bring you some coffee, milord?"

"That won't be necessary," he said abruptly. He paused too long. "Thank you," he said stiffly.

Soon he heard the children's excited voices and their footsteps on the stairs. He stood as the door opened, the children bursting in in front of their governess.

Anna Kate looked lovely, in an azure carriage

dress, covered with a white pelisse with azure trim. The colors brought out the blue of her eyes and the rose of her cheeks. Her health contrasted rudely with Diana's ill health. He took a deep breath to keep from noting the contrast aloud.

The children looked extremely healthy too. He had to scold himself. Did he not want them to be hale and hearty, just because Diana was not? He knew no one would countenance his strange sensibilities if he were to express them.

"Milord," Anna said quietly.

Quill didn't bother to correct her today. He did not like to hear her call him that, but he'd done too much correcting at their last meeting.

He had the feeling she was reining in her usual exuberance. Had he made her afraid of him? He was saddened by the thought. The fact that he was older, more mature than she, did not signify he could judge her youthfulness.

"Anna," he said expansively, "you look lovely."

She flushed, then stammered. "Why, thank you."

Mary, no sign of her earlier illness apparent, put her hands on diminutive hips, then came very close to stomping one black-kid shod foot. "Well, of course, she looks lovely. She is bee-yootiful."

"Now, Mary," Anna corrected gently, "mind your manners, dear."

Mary tossed shining brown ringlets off her face and tipped her nose in the air. Quill thought he could read her small-female mind: You adults may correct me, but it will not change my mind.

He grinned. "Are you children ready to meet Brutus the Wonder Horse?"

Paul nodded. "Spot on! Where is he?"

Anna smiled in apology for her charges. They were being reared much more gently than most children, so they tended to behave familiarly even with strangers. "Paul, be patient. Lord Wentworth will show you."

"I see you have your wraps," Quill said. "It is a bit sharp outside still, although fair and bright. Come along." He put his hand out to Mary, who took his large, tanned one confidently. He gestured to Paul and Anna Kate to precede them. "Brutus is tied right out in front. I do imagine, however, we should move to the mews so you can see him do his tricks more readily. He may frighten passersby."

"Ooh," Mary said. "Is he scary?"

Quill laughed. "Not really. He is merely very large. When he takes to dancing about, he seems even larger."

"Your horse dances?" Paul said. The wrinkles on his freckled nose indicated to Quill that he, Paul, did not think much of dancing himself.

"Oh, my, yes. He is quite the young man about town. All gentlemen learn to dance, so that they can squire young ladies around." He felt rather than heard the collective sighs of Anna and Mary. He'd just scored a point for the distaff side of society.

And it hadn't hurt at all. Perhaps he should listen more to his own mother and help out the marry-off-Anna campaign. And it was like a campaign, he realized, as much as any Wellington plotted to defeat the French.

When they reached Brutus, the large animal lifted his head, nodding it several times. "He is greeting you," Quill said. "Brutus, may I introduce to you Miss Mary Stanfield, Master Paul Stanfield, and Miss Forsythe." Again the horse seemed to nod in greeting. "But Brutus, watch Paul closely," Quill said. "He may try to steal you away from me." With that Brutus shoved Paul in the shoulder, forcefully but not enough to knock the boy over.

Paul began to laugh. "You are right, milord. I may steal him away!"

Quill picked up Mary to swing her onto the horse's back, then placed Paul behind her. "Mind your manners, Brute. You have precious cargo."

The children were beaming as Quill led Brutus around to the mews behind the Stanfields' house. He noted Anna was smiling too, although she kept her head docilely lowered and would not look him in the eye.

He knew he still needed to make amends to her. Perhaps he could make up for his boorishness last week. "You asked about Diana in your note."

Anna nodded.

He stopped, put a hand on her shoulder, and turned her so she was facing him. "She is not well."

Death in Exile

She covered her mouth with one hand. Tears started in her eyes, those improbably large, bluebell-hued eyes. "I...I am so saddened to hear that." She dropped her gaze. "I do pray, milord, that you will allow me to come visit her. Perhaps I could help with her care."

"It is not necessary. My mother is in town to help."

Her cheeks flamed. "But..."

He cursed himself for a fool. "I tender my apology, Anna Kate. Of course you may come. I wanted to spare you, but I see you care about her too."

"Of course I care!" she snapped. "What do you take me for?"

Quill stiffened. At that moment, however, before he could speak, Mary spoke up from her perch high on the horse's wide back. "What tricks does this horse do? Anna Kate said he does tricks."

"Tricks, yes, he does tricks." The old crossness was back in his tone.

Mary teared up, and Anna stepped forward to pat her hand. "Do not fret, Mary, dear. He will not bite. He only barks."

Blood rose to his darkened face. "I apologize, Miss Mary. I do have a tendency to bark. I mean nothing—mostly—by it."

"Your tone is still cold," Anna said acerbically.

"And yours is—" Quill bit his tongue. She was not going to anger him today, no matter how shrewish she became. He wished he could shake the widgeon. Here he'd started this outing with only the best of intentions. He gritted his teeth and leaned over close to her. "It is in truth beyond belief how you irritate a man!"

No more coy glances, no more bowed head. She threw her head back, pert nose in the air, neck stiff. "Only irritable ones," she snapped.

He nearly laughed aloud. "Touché, Miss Mouth." With the use of the word, he glanced at her mouth. Pursed, it looked quite kissable. What would that be like, to kiss her? He shook his head to clear it. "None of that now."

Color rushing to her face, as though she knew precisely what he was thinking, she said, "I beg your pardon!"

"Oh, what now? You are the most tiresome widgeon on the face of God's green earth." He realized he was shouting and the children were staring at him open-mouthed. "I came here trying to make amends for my boorish behavior of the other day, with my hat in my hand, and you must behave the harridan!"

The fair skin around Anna's mouth turned white. Now he knew he had really angered her. "You think you cut quite a dash, do you not, milord, and all the ladies must grovel in admiration at your feet? Well, you have come to the wrong lady for that!"

"Lady? No lady acts in such a way!"

Picking up her skirts with both hands, Anna

Kate swished around and marched out of the mews. "I will send the groom for the children. I do trust you can keep them safe for a few moments!"

He watched her go, half glad, half devastated. Curse her! Just what did she think she was about anyway? What a missish young lady, throwing fits like this, and nearly in public too! Wait until he told his mother...

With thought of his mother, Quill suddenly saw in his mind's eye just what he had done, just how very provoking his good lady mother might consider him to have been. He groaned. "Now I'm in for it," he said to the air.

"And rightly so," Mary said, impertinent. "You were quite rude to our dear Miss Anna."

Paul poked her shoulder. "Mary, hush!"

Quill looked at Paul. The child's eyes were wide with fear. Perhaps the boy imagined he, Quill, would be as cross with them. He needed to apologize. He patted Mary's knee, at his shoulder height since she was sitting on Brutus. "You are right," he said sincerely. "I will need to make my apologies to her later. Please forgive me?"

Mary beamed, happy to oblige. Paul still looked frightened.

"I was very impolitic in my speech, Paul. Please forget I ever behaved in such a way. I do hope you escape having the sort of temper I am cursed with." With those words he smiled gently, to erase the concern on the boy's face.

Schunk

At last Paul's shoulders relaxed and his jaw
unclenched. Then Quill knew all was well, at least
until the next time he lost his temper with their
beloved governess.

Chapter 6

Anna Kate began to run once she had rounded the corner of the mews. Tears streamed down her face. Oh, how he could set her off! And now, with this latest farrago, she would not be able to go visit Diana.

Her tears grew stronger. She slowed her pace because she could not see. Once she reached the front of the house, she began to hiccough. He was maddening!

Fresh anger helped dry her tears. She paused at the bottom of the steps, her hand on the railing. Across the lane a man stood under a bare plane tree. Was he watching her, or was she imagining things? Of medium height, with broad shoulders and a black bushy beard on a wide face, with fat red cheeks, he seemed to be pretending no interest in her, but surely he had been looking at her just seconds ago.

Was another man talking with him? The second man had his back to Anna, so she couldn't see his face. He walked off, and she could still see only his back. He was tall and slim, elegantly dressed. Another stranger watching her?

Why would anyone watch her? Her imagination must be playing up.

Purposing to forget her wild fancies, she decided she would call on Diana without Quill's permission or leave. She would merely go and present her card, and Mr. High and Mighty Quillen Rossiter could just go hang! He could not keep her from her duty to Diana.

She slipped into the house and up the stairs to her room. She would once again have to repair the ravages his hatefulness wreaked on her face. If only her face didn't blotch so.

Once in her room, Anna Kate castigated herself. *Why has he so much power to overset me? I must gain control over my sensitivities so he cannot control me.*

She quickly washed her face. She couldn't leave the children unsupervised. Dashing down the two flights of stairs, she reminded herself she had to go see Diana. And right away.

Once she reached the turn in the wide stairs above the foyer, she looked down. Quill and the children were entering and Constance standing there to help Mary and Paul out of their wraps.

Mary's high spirits bubbled out. "The big horse can count and say yes and no and everything, Mother."

"More importantly," Paul added, his face somber, "he obeys instantly, like backing up or side-stepping." He turned to Quill and asked, "Do you think I could teach our pony things like that?"

Constance laughed and shook her head. "My goodness, children, let the man be."

Quill smiled, his charm now back in place. "They're not bothering me. I'm glad to see them appreciate what a good horse can do." To Paul he said, "I do not know whether you can teach your pony all the things Brutus can do. She may be too old. It would take much time and patience, but there is no harm in trying. I can show you a few pointers about how to get your pony to learn each part of any given trick."

"Now?" Paul asked.

"Now," Quill answered. "It's starting to rain, so perhaps you should put on some boots, to keep your feet neat."

Paul nodded. "I'll be right back."

"What about me?" Mary asked, petulant.

"If your mother says you may go, I will be glad of your company."

Anna Kate still stood on the wide landing above the group below. She hoped no one saw her there as she spied on them. Mr. Rossiter, Lord Wentworth, treated Mary differently from the way he treated Paul, more condescendingly. Was that good or bad? She wasn't sure. She didn't think she liked it, however. Mary should naturally be included in the plans to train the pony as much as Paul was, should she not?

Anna Kate wanted to stamp her foot. Confused, frustrated, pulled in several directions at once, she realized she wished she was being included in the horse-training plans, as Paul was. She wanted to be on equal footing with Quill, the way things used to be, when they were young.

She sighed. She refused to break in on the group. If he did not think to include her, so be it.

Tilting her head up, nose high at an uncharacteristically haughty angle, she decided this was the right time to go see Diana. At least he wouldn't be at home to correct her every word, her every move.

The tableau below her swirled, then broke up, with Quill taking the children back to the mews. Constance stopped them on their way out the front door. "Surely it is quicker and easier to go through the kitchens, if you don't mind the informality, Quill."

"That will be fine, thank you." He smiled again. Anna Kate's heart tipped over. He really had a charming smile. So why did he not cultivate his charming manner toward her?

She stomped her foot. So irritating! *Let it roll off you, like water off a duck's back*, she heard her father's voice say.

Good advice, Papa, good advice. Now if I could only follow it.

CHAPTER 7

Once Quill and the children were gone, Anna Kate quickly descended the stairs to join Constance, who was plucking withered chrysanthemums from a bronze, gold, and green fall arrangement at the foot of the stairs.

"Constance, I apologize."

She turned to stare at Anna. "Whatever for?"

"For not being here to manage the children." She lowered her head. Heat flooded her cheeks. "He...I...he oversets me so. I do not know how he does it, but he makes me feel a perfect ninnyhammer."

Constance smiled. "By 'he' I assume you mean Lord Wentworth." She took one of Anna Kate's hands in hers. "Your hand is freezing. He must really affect you."

"I feel so ridiculous around him, as though I were still thirteen. I fancy he thinks me still only thirteen."

Schunk

Constance patted her hand. "I think the children are fine. He seems quite kind. And he is overwhelmingly handsome, is he not?"

"Oh! Do you think so? I hadn't noticed." She blushed again. Another thing to confess! What was she coming to? She changed the subject. "I want to go visit Diana. Can you spare me for a short time?"

"Of course, dear heart, but no going out on your own this time. I will ask Travis to accompany you and have the carriage brought 'round for you. There's a weather change in the air, and I do not want my dear Anna out in a downpour."

Anna put her cheek up against Constance's. "Thank you. You are so kind. I can go alone, though. No need to take Travis away from her sewing."

"She has finished the children's Christmas clothes. I can spare her. You must be accompanied in public now."

Anna's heart fell. No more solo trips to the shops, no more walks in the park. So dull.

Anna Kate hoped the drive would soothe her jangled nerves. Travis smiled sweetly but did not speak after answering her greeting. She looked so young, surely only Anna's own age, to be responsible for the wardrobe of such a prestigious family. Her black hair was pulled severely back from her long face, her large brown eyes reminding Anna of a young doe.

As the carriage pulled out of the Stanfields' lane, Anna Kate looked back and saw the same strange man she had noticed earlier. Surely he was not watching her. "There is that man again."

"Again?" Travis repeated.

"Yes, I'd noticed him earlier. So odd. It is a bit too chill outside for someone to be taking the air." Yet why would anyone watch her? She shook her head and told herself she was being a goose.

Dismissing the man from her mind, she sat back and planned how she would ask to see Diana. Surely no one would refuse her entrance merely because Quill disliked her.

The butler let her in and led her to the drawing room, where Quill's mother, Eleanor Rossiter, Lady Wentworth, soon joined her. "Anna Kate, my dear, pray sit down." She gestured to a crimson brocade sofa. "You have been on my mind," she said warmly.

"Thank you for seeing me, Lady Wentworth. I have been distressed by Diana's situation but unable to get away because of my duties."

At the word *duties*, Eleanor Rossiter winced. "Oh, my. I am so concerned—should your mother's daughter be working as a governess?"

Anna stiffened. "If it is good enough for my father's daughter, I believe it is good enough for my mother's." She covered her mouth. "Oh, dear, please forgive me. My tongue keeps running away with itself. I fear it is a dreadful failing in me."

Eleanor Rossiter smiled. "That is what Quill tells me."

Anna gasped. "He has told you that about me?"

"But it is good that he notices you again. He thought he had outgrown you. At least now you two can renew your acquaintance."

"But he despises me!"

Eleanor smiled. "You think so? But you did not come to talk to me. You want to see Diana. She is not well. I am very concerned about her emotional state. And she is not eating. Perhaps you can cheer her."

"I pray so."

"Come. It's nearly time for her next bath. I order one every two hours now. The water seems to cool her and soothe her nerves. She still has not told me much about her experiences. Perhaps she will tell you."

Anna followed Lady Wentworth up the winding stairs. She wanted to examine all the *objets d'art* in the foyer and in small insets in the wall along the stairs, but she did not dare. She did not want Lady Wentworth to know her excessive interest in all things relating to her son the earl. It was surely shameful of her.

She wanted to tiptoe once they reached the ivory room. Mahogany woods and painted red roses on the ivory coverlet delineated the huge bed where Diana lay. Anna's hands were freezing, and her stomach lurched. What if Diana didn't want to see her? What if her visit upset Diana? What if Diana found her as childish as Quill did, what if she despised her childhood friend also?

Once they reached the bed, Eleanor leaned over to lay her wrist against Diana's cheek. Next to the bed, on the bed stand, sat a cooling bowl of broth. Struck by how pale her friend looked, Anna steeled herself to conceal her dismay.

Diana's eyelids fluttered open, first showing alarm, then, once she recognized Anna, a warm welcome that melted Anna's heart. "Anna Kate," she whispered, reaching out to take Anna's hand, "it is so good to see you."

Leaning over her, Anna placed a gentle kiss on her forehead. "It is so good to see you too, darling Diana. I have been so worried about you."

Eleanor placed a small chair next to the bed. "I'll let you two chat for a bit, then return to give your bath, Diana." Diana grimaced. "I know you don't like the baths, but I think they help you."

"They chill me so."

"Because of your fever. But I am sure you are better for some time after they are over."

"Perhaps," she said softly.

Anna sat next to Diana's bed, still holding her hand. "Can you eat a bit for me? I will spoon only a small amount into your mouth at a time."

Diana shook her head vigorously. "No. I cannot eat. I will lose it all if I try."

Anna sighed but did not pursue the issue. "Tell me what has happened to you. It is dreadful... I am so sorry. My heart aches for you."

Diana closed her eyes and said nothing for a moment. Anna examined her friend's appearance, cringing inwardly at the yellowish-green bruises on the long, swan-like neck.

"This tale will distress you. But I must tell someone. I feel sure Henry will discover me before too long."

"No!"

"Yes. You don't know what he's like. Henry acted so loving to me before the marriage, but he truly hates me. It is dreadful to be despised so." She gulped back tears. "He is cruel. I would not have thought it possible." She pressed shaking fingers over her mouth to stem the sobs.

"Please, you can wait until you are well," Anna told her.

Diana took a deep breath. "No, I must tell you now. It began soon after we moved into Stafford Hall. You know he took me away from Andover as soon as he could. He did not want my friends to be able to see his treatment of me." Her voice deepened with bitterness.

"I am so sorry. I didn't know."

"He has used up all of my money, except a small inheritance from my grandmother. He cannot get at it, so that is why he has turned against me. The small pouch—you still have it?"

Death in Exile

"Yes! But what is it?"

"Not now. Just keep it safe. His brutality the past five months has been extreme, but I have refused to sign any more money over to him." She touched her side, the place that had started bleeding that Friday when they found each other. It was only days before, but it seemed like weeks. "He finally, about ten days ago, became so enraged he knocked me to the floor and repeatedly kicked me. He was so angry, he forgot to avoid letting others see what he did to me. That time we had witnesses. The next day he let go both my maid Hannah and the housekeeper Mrs. Mathers. They were without employ because of me. And now Mathers is dead." At this point she sobbed deeply. "Do you think me so wrong to have refused him, dear Anna? The law says so. Everything I have must belong to my husband."

"No, of course, I do not. You are brave and fine." She squeezed Diana's hand.

"He beat me near to death that time ten days ago. And then two days ago he reopened this wound in my side, so I ran." She wrung her hands. "I didn't know what else to do. Because I continued to refuse, he plots to have me imprisoned and transported, he hopes, to Australia." She laughed humorlessly. "I do not know why he doesn't just have me confined to Newgate where I will die quickly—spite, I think, to drag it out and humiliate me in the process. Even if I die, he still will not be able to touch my inheritance, which will go to my second cousin in Hampshire. He may believe the deadly trip to Australia will be a worse torment even than a damp, cold cell."

"Oh, Diana. What can I do for you? How can I help?"

Diana tried to smile, but the skin on her face stretched tight in pain. "Just be my friend, continue to be my true Anna. Keep the packet safe that I gave you. Please tell no one—you'll be safer. If I should die…"

"No!"

"If I die, give the packet to Quill. He can deliver it to my cousin Jenny Marquardt—he knows her."

Abashed, Anna felt she couldn't argue with Diana in the precarious state she was in. "I'll do my best."

"And pray for me, please. I believe…I do believe that will help me."

"Diana, I will; I have been praying for you already." She wondered whether it had helped. She could not see any results yet, except that Diana was still alive.

Lady Wentworth entered at that moment. "The water is ready for your bath, Diana." She examined Diana's face closely. "I do believe Anna Kate's visit has helped you some."

Anna darted a glance at the older woman's face. On what did she base such a judgment? Diana looked dreadful.

"Yes," Diana whispered. "She is a big help to me. Do come again, dear Anna."

"I will." Anna leaned over to kiss Diana's cheek. It burned with fever. Anna choked back her tears. Would Diana survive this? To Lady Wentworth, who looked tired, she said, "May I help with the bathing?"

"No, dear, you run along. I will have the help of Harriet and Trude. They are good, strong girls used to lifting wet laundry. But please do come again."

With that Anna knew she'd been dismissed. She left slowly, her heart aching for Diana.

CHAPTER 8

Travis, Constance's seamstress, awaited Anna Kate in the carriage. "Miss Anna," she said, her brow furrowed, "there's that strange man watching the house again. Do you think you should tell the earl?"

"Why, you're right. What on earth is going on?"

Just then a second carriage pulled in front of Quill's house. Anna didn't recognize it. When the tall, blond man, dressed in a navy jacket, buff breeches, and shining black boots, hopped down from the landau, she knew immediately who it was. Lucas Cranford, baron of Breckin, Diana's childhood sweetheart.

She knocked on the roof of the carriage. "Stop, please. Take us back to the Wentworths'." Gathering her reticule and her long skirts, she left the carriage once it had stopped.

Lucas was already at the door, raising the brass knocker. "Lucas," she called, "what are you doing here?"

Schunk

"Looking for Diana. Have you seen her? I thought perhaps Quill would know..."

Anna quickly put a finger up to her lips, then looked around for the man who seemed to be watching. He had left his spot and was walking briskly away from Quill's house. "Shh," she said. "There may be listening ears." Putting her hand on his arm, she led him into the house once the door was opened by Randall, Quill's butler. "May we come in, Randall? It is a matter of some urgency."

At that moment Quill entered the foyer from a baize-covered door in the hall. "Lucas! To what do we owe the honor of a visit?" He bowed slightly to Anna. "And hello again, Anna Kate."

His voice was low and slightly husky when he spoke her name, his eyes, she thought, warm. She did not understand him at all, but her heart welcomed the change in him.

"I am looking for Diana. I met her odious husband in the Two Swans on Friday and he asked me to Stafford Hall for tea. When I arrived, no one was there to greet me, only some poor devil of a butler shaking in his boots. Said he hadn't seen Diana for days. I went back Saturday and yesterday too. Still no one. The butler's cornered-rat demeanor indicated to me something was very wrong." He gritted his teeth. "I decided you might know what."

Quill glanced upstairs. Anna could almost see wheels turning in his head as he thought briefly about whether he should tell Lucas. "She is here," he said at last. "She is not well, I fear, abused as she has been by Henry. Can you steel yourself to see her and not show your shock?"

"As bad as all that?" Lucas asked, his handsome features twisted.

Quill gestured to Anna. "Will you come say hello to Diana again?"

So he must already have spoken to his mother about her visit. Had Lady Wentworth praised her in some way, to soften his attitude toward her? She shook her head. "No, I must return home. They will be concerned at how long I have been gone. I will return tomorrow, however, if that is acceptable, milord."

He grinned. "No milording me, now. Yes, do come again." He led her to the door.

Once Anna was outside, she remembered the strange man. Stopping on the top step, she looked around. He was nowhere to be seen. Was he spying on her? Perhaps, but it was Lucas's arrival that had sent him scurrying. Oh, she wished she knew what was going on. Even after hearing Diana's story of how Henry had beaten her, it was difficult for Anna to countenance the idea of one human being treating another so. Was the stranger an emissary for Henry? Somehow that seemed plausible.

She needed to tell Quill about the man. She turned back to raise the knocker once more. Blushing at the surprise on Randall's face, she apologized. "Please ask Lord Wentworth if I may speak to him one more time."

While waiting in the drawing room, Anna sat on a small love seat and gripped her hands together until they ached. She was afraid of Quill, but more so, she was frightened for Diana.

His face bland, Quill entered the room and stood across from where Anna sat. "Yes?"

His looks nearly overwhelmed her. He was darkly handsome, and his eyes deep and intelligent. His full lower lip made her long for a kiss, even a short, avuncular one.

She nearly stuttered as she spoke. But she forced herself to be bold. "I hate to disturb you, mi...Quill, but I feel you should know. There was a strange man outside Constance and Ansten's house this morning while you were with the children, then he was here again when I came to visit Diana."

"A strange man?" he repeated.

She quickly described him, with his round face and large black beard. "He was quite distinctive, not the sort of person one would ignore. He did not act furtive in the least, yet once Lucas arrived and I spoke to him, the man disappeared up your lane." She paused, biting her lip as she thought. "Perhaps it is you he watches. He must have left when you arrived. Did you come in from the mews?"

"Yes," he said slowly, his brow furrowed as he pondered her news.

When he said no more, Anna rose from the love seat and took three steps toward him. "I need to go. I merely wanted you to know about the man. Diana told me Henry will find her before long."

Quill scowled, pulling on his upper lip with thumb and forefinger. "We must move her."

Panic filled Anna's heart. "But where? Please, Quill, do not move her where I cannot see her!"

He looked at her as though he had not realized she was standing there. "She must be moved to a place where Henry will not know the individuals sheltering her. This will take some thought." He stepped closer to her, then stood beside her, his hand on her back. "You need to run along. I will notify you of her residence once I find someplace safe. Do not tell anyone where she is."

She stiffened. "Of course not. Do you think I would put her in jeopardy?"

Still absent-minded, he shook his head, "No, of course not. But I must have time to think." Once they were in the foyer, Quill rang for Randall. When the butler arrived, he said, "Please show Miss Forsythe out. And if any strangers come asking for Mrs. Rutledge, you know nothing."

"Yes, sir." Randall spoke smartly, almost militarily.

With no farewell, Quill started up the stairs, three steps at a stride. Anna knew she'd been forgotten already. Once again she figured that Quill was in love with Diana. The pang that thought gave her pierced a corner of her heart. At least now, knowing he would never return her own affection, she could quash any hopes she foolishly encouraged for her own chances with him.

And with what Diana had suffered at the hands of Henry Rutledge, she was entitled, Anna knew, to something much, much better.

Once outside she glanced at Lucas's carriage. His presence would confuse issues if Quill was in love with Diana. But she had no doubt Quill could win Diana's heart from anyone, even Lucas.

She hurried to her own carriage. She had been gone from the Stanfields' for much too long. Travis was still sitting patiently inside the carriage.

"Has the stranger returned?" Anna asked.

"No, miss, I have not seen him."

Anna sighed. "I don't know whether that's good or bad. Well, let's return home. There is nothing more I can do here." On the way home she continued thinking about Diana's condition. She felt powerless to help. Then she remembered the old cook at Diana's grandmother's home. Cook—she thought her name was Jemima White—made the most delicious beef soup, heavy with meat and laced with egg and ginger. Cook swore it was healing.

Anna resolved to make some and bring it back to Diana. Perhaps she could entice her friend to eat some of it.

She and Travis returned to a silent, heavy household. Travis excused herself and returned to her room.

Constance looked distraught, her face drawn

and pinched. "Oh, Anna, I'm so glad you're here," she said, drawing her into the parlor. "Mme Vero is here with sad news."

"What is it?" she asked, alarmed.

"I'll let her tell you."

When Anna entered the room, Mme Vero, who looked as if she'd been up all night, rose and came to her. Her face was splotched from crying, and her hair and dress were in disarray. "You must tell me who that woman was that Mister Sumner saw at my shop."

"Why? What's wrong?"

"Come sit, both of you," Constance said, directing them both to a small love seat. "I've sent for tea."

Alarmed for all of them now, Anna took Mme Vero's hands, which were like ice. "What happened?"

"Two men we didn't know came to my apartment early this morning. They pounded so hard they woke the neighbors. Blaine—Mr. Sumner—answered the door. The men grabbed him and threw him up against the wall. I was so dumbfounded I couldn't think what to do.

"They kept saying, 'Where is she, where is she?'

"'Where is who?' I asked, but they didn't answer for the longest time. At last they said, 'The woman you treated at the milliner shop on Friday.'"

Mme Vero fumbled up her sleeve for a handkerchief. "As you know, neither of us knew her name. I told them that, and they refused to believe me, and they proceeded to beat Blaine nearly to death. He is at death's door even now at my apartment. I've called in his friend, who is the best surgeon in town. Chaddowes worked over him for hours, and he tried to tell me to have hope, but I don't know—Blaine looks so awful and cannot speak! What if he never speaks again?" She covered her face with her hands and began to cry. "They beat his head so severely he was bleeding from his ears. What if he cannot hear now?"

Anna put her arms around her. "I'm so sorry, I'm so sorry."

Vero raised her head and looked at Anna, clutching at her hands in desperation. "Who is she, and why is she worth so much?"

Anna pulled back. "I...I cannot say, Madame. I am so sorry. Mr. Sumner saved her life but may lose his? Oh, the beast will pay for this!"

"You know who is behind this?" the older woman asked, hope rising in her face.

"I think so. He will kill her if he finds her." Anna pulled out of Mme Vero's grasp and rose to pace around the room.

"But Blaine! What if they come back?"

"I must talk to...someone about this. She will soon be out of reach of the man." She crossed the room, back to where Mme Vero sat and knelt beside her. "I'm so sorry your friend has been hurt. I'll do my best to see that the Beast is brought to justice for this."

Then a thought came to her. "The two men. What did they look like?"

"One looked a common footpad, the other quite elegant. They weren't of the same class at all."

"Was one a big man with a round face and a bushy black beard?"

Mme Vero frowned. "No, neither man looked like that."

Disappointed, Anna rose and began to pace again. At that point tea was brought in, and she and Constance did their best to get Mme Vero to drink tea with two sugar cubes in it, for shock, and to eat a bit, to keep her strength up.

Once she ate a bit, Mme Vero rose to take her leave. "I must get back to him."

"Do you have a carriage?" Constance asked.

"No, I can walk."

"Oh, we won't hear of that. I'll call to have our carriage come around to take you back."

"No, that would take too long!"

"Not long at all," Constance said, her voice soothing as ever.

Once Mme Vero was seen into the carriage, Constance turned to Anna. "What is going on?"

"Oh, Constance, it's better if I don't tell you. This is something Lord Wentworth is working on, and I cannot tell anyone what it is. Please bear with me?"

Constance looked after the departing carriage.

"All right. But this is very serious. It's Rutledge and your friend, Diana, right?"

"Don't ask me now, I beg of you!"

At last Constance agreed, but unwillingly. "This must be a very dangerous situation for you too. If you don't tell anyone, who knows what they'll do to you."

"But Quill knows. I'll go back, once the carriage returns, and tell him about this latest attack. The Beast is desperate, I know."

"I'll pray for you all," Constance said, hurt in her face and voice. "I guess that's all I can do."

Quill found Lucas Cranford cooling his elegant heels outside Diana's room. He was leaning casually against the wall, his eyes fixed on her closed door.

"They tell me she is getting a bath to reduce her fever."

"Yes, my mother believes it helps her rest." He scowled, then began pacing in the hall. "That was Anna Kate back at the door. She told me of a stranger who has been watching, first at the Stanfields where she stays, then here. The man left abruptly about the time you and I arrived." He stopped his pacing and described the man to Lucas. "Does he sound familiar?"

Lucas shook his head. "No, not at all."

"Tell me again about your meeting with Rutledge. It was Friday, you say?"

Lucas repeated the details of his exchange with Rutledge. "It was all I could do to keep from throttling the man. I swear he was up to something, Quill. What, I do not know."

"Diana had already escaped and was here by the time he approached you at the Two Swans. I would definitely say he was up to something." Quill resumed his pacing. "I must find another place for her to stay while she is ill, someplace he cannot associate with me, or with you. I hate to tell even one more person about her. Too many know already."

Lady Wentworth opened the door at that moment. "You may come in now, gentlemen, but I pray, do not stay long. Visits cheer her, but they also tire her."

"Yes, my lady," Lucas said earnestly. "I will take care not to fatigue her."

He entered cautiously, as though afraid his very footsteps would disturb her. His face blanched when he saw the weakened condition she was in, as well as the bruises and the cuts. "Diana?" he said softly.

She turned to look at him, and her eyes widened. "Lucas! How nice to see you!" Then her manner changed. "But you may not be glad to see me, after the way you were left nearly at the altar. I must tell you, it was not my doing that I did not appear." At this, she began to cry. "He would not let..."

Lucas's face twisted in pain. "Oh, dear Diana!

87

How could he...? You're out of his reach now, and getting you well is all that matters. Please don't cry!" He picked up one of her hands and kissed it.

To Quill he looked to be in nearly as much pain as Diana. Eleanor crossed to the far side of the bed and, picking up a white linen cloth, dampened it and began to wipe Diana's face. She began to croon some low song that reminded Quill of his childhood illnesses and his mother's loving, caressing way with him when he was ill. He both loved and respected his mother for her good character and strong will.

As he watched, the image of Anna Kate rose in his mind. He began to compare her with his mother. She was merely young, as his mother had pointed out. But with age would she gain Eleanor's quiet elegance? Diana had it now, had had it from childhood on.

Yet it was Anna he warmed to, not Diana, as much as he valued the lovely heiress, who was now in dire need of protection. He returned to the task before him. "Mother," he said when Eleanor had calmed Diana and rejoined him at the door. "I need to move Diana to another house. Can you recommend someone who will be discreet?"

Eleanor thought briefly, then directed Quill out of the room. "Let them visit alone for a few moments." She closed the door behind her. "Perhaps Cassandra Austen. The fun we used to have at their childhood home, acting out plays for the adults!

Cassandra is a dedicated nurse, she and her sister Jane. In fact, I'm sure they are presently visiting their brother Edward's. He was adopted by the Knights, you know, to be their heir at Godmersham."

"Wait. You mean Jane Austen, the author? How could she find time to nurse Diana now, as successful as her books have become?"

"She doesn't write all the time. But I meant Cassandra primarily. She can be trusted, as can Jane, to be discreet. Their aunt, Jane Leigh-Austen, was once falsely accused by a shopkeeper of stealing a bit of lace. Cassandra and Jane will understand the situation." She paused to think a moment.

"I'm sure that Cassandra is in Kent at Godmersham House with her brother's family at the moment. It would take some time to reach her, but I could send Coachman John. He is quite a horseman."

Quill shook his head. "No, you may need him here. I will find Toby Esterby. He's the soul of discretion." He began a mad dash down the back stairs. "Tell Lucas I'll return soon."

On his way out the back door, he grabbed his cloak from the settle in the kitchen where he had left it earlier. He didn't speak to the cook or to Mrs. Godwin, the housekeeper. They didn't expect him to, as pressed as he was and as cool as he usually acted with them.

CHAPTER 9

Quill dashed out of the house and into the mews where he kept Brutus stabled. Coachman John came out to check on the noise when his master ran across the cobbles. "What is it, milord?"

"Has Brutus been unsaddled yet?" he asked.

"Yes, sir, and cooled down and curried."

"Good for the cool down at least. Can you re-saddle him? I must leave quickly." He trusted John, but even so, he dared not tell him about the errand he was on.

Once the large, gleaming black stallion was brought out to him, Quill turned to John. "Have you noticed a bearded stranger around, or anyone asking odd questions?"

John shook his head, then said, "Wait. There was a man soon after you arrived this noon. He wasn't bearded though, but high-tone and dapper. He asked whether you had been visiting Jane Rutledge. I did not know who Jane Rutledge was, so of course I said no. Did I do wrong?"

Quill reached out to pat him on the shoulder. "You did precisely right. You know nothing, you understand? Can you play stupid, even perhaps as though you do not understand plain English?"

John grinned. He was quite a wholesome-looking lad, of perhaps twenty years or so. His father had served Quill's own father for many years. Now he tugged at his cornshock-colored forelock, stuck his upper teeth out a fraction of an inch over his bottom lip, and said, slurring his speech, "Sirrah, I don' git yer meanin'." He looked the complete country bumpkin.

"Keep it up," Quill said, swinging up on his horse. "There'll be an extra fillip in your pay next week."

Thunder rolled over his head as he cantered out of the mews. He shivered in the north wind that caught him when he rounded the buildings at the end of the lane, leaving him out in the open, at the wind's mercy. It was the weather change they'd expected for some days.

Large cold drops of rain caught him full in the face. As the rain fell more strongly, he began to wish he'd taken his landau. But no, Brutus would get him to his destination faster.

Toby had told him he was staying at the Two Swans. That was where Rutledge had found Lucas; Quill would have to be very sure the swine was not close by when he gave Toby the commission.

Death in Exile

Rutledge must be completely desperate, Quill thought, to have approached Lucas as he had on Friday. That out-of-character invitation to tea was a ploy to find out whether Lucas knew where Diana was.

Quill was at a disadvantage. He had no idea what sort of equipage Henry had, nor who his men were, other than Walters, the bailiff. Could Walters be the bearded man Anna described?

Once he drew up to the Two Swans, he had his answer. He saw Rutledge supervising the lading of his carriage. The carriage was distinctive, painted a black enamel with three white plumes on the side. A seat rose up high behind the enclosed interior. It had to have cost the moon.

He was talking to a bearded man, who had his hand out. It wasn't Walters, but it was likely the man Henry had hired to trace Diana.

"You didn't see her there?" Rutledge was saying.

Henry didn't notice Quill, who decided to leave Brutus on the street behind the inn and to approach the Two Swans from the other side, out of Rutledge's range of vision.

Rutledge sounded as though he was trying to avoid paying the man for his work. Quill snorted. That seemed typical of the scoundrel.

Quill slipped in the side entrance to the taproom. Looking around him for Toby, he waved to the barman, an old chum of Toby's from his village, who was now laconically wiping off the bar. Quill crossed the room and gestured to Blinkers to approach him.

"What'll ya have, guv'nor?" Blinkers smiled warmly, revealing a large gap between stained front teeth. He was an ugly man, but he was pleasant enough.

"Have you seen Toby around today?"

Blinkers scratched at the three-days' growth on his chin. "Esterby? You're the third bloke to be askin' for 'im today."

"Is that toad Rutledge asking questions here?"

"I don't know his name, but there's sure been a toad hangin' about. Friend of yers?"

"Don't tell him I've been here if he should ask. I suspect, however, that he's on his way out of town now."

"Good riddance." Blinkers went back to wiping the bar.

"Toby?"

"Oh, right. Second floor, third room. He should be up there. He drank himself a right headsplitter last night."

"Oh, great," Quill said.

With no time to waste, he took the stairs three at a time. He needed to return home in case Rutledge decided to pay a call.

Pounding on the door, Quill called Toby's name as quietly as he could. At last the door opened to reveal a red-eyed, red-haired scarecrow in his long johns. He was struggling to pull on a dirty shirt. "If it wasn't you, Quill, I'd murder you. I have a beastly head."

"Serves you right for exceeding your limit," Quill said, brushing Toby aside and entering the room. "I need your help. What does it take to get you decent after a drunk?"

Toby collapsed on the edge of the bed and held his head in his hands. "I don't know. I've never had one quite like this before. It was pure gin."

"Toby," Quill said somberly, "this may be a matter of life and death. You must help me. I'll have Blinkers send up coffee and toast—please get to my house as soon as you can. I must return. Rutledge may be on Diana's trail."

"That clutch-fisted, rat-faced, pox-ridden..."

"Enough, Toby. Anything besides coffee and toast?"

He moaned. "Just coffee. My stomach won't stomach food." He grimaced at his pun. "I'll be right along."

Quill hesitated a moment. "You won't go back to bed."

"No, of course not, man! I'll come within thirty minutes."

His eyes were clearer by this point, so Quill believed him. "Thanks," Quill said and left him to get dressed.

He departed from the inn the same way he had entered. He walked purposefully around a large

farm wagon being unloaded of potatoes and cab-
bages at the kitchen door, then peered around the
edge of the building. Rutledge and his coach were
gone. So was the bearded man. Quill could see him
walking away, about a block from the Two Swans
on the other side of the street. Rain was falling
steadily and coldly. The horses on the street steamed
from the temperature change. Perhaps the bad
weather would slow Rutledge, forestall his plans,
whatever they were.

He looked again at the man walking away from
the inn and wondered whether he could get useful
information from him. A detective, perhaps? If such
he was, should he pursue the man? If Rutledge, who
was known for his stinginess, stiffed him his fee,
the man would surely spill what he knew.

Quill decided against following him, however.
Right now getting back to his house to forestall
Rutledge was the most important thing on his
agenda.

He swung easily up on Brutus, who was eager
to get home. "You don't like standing about in the
rain when you have a full bag of oats awaiting you
at home, do you?" Quill asked the horse. Brutus
snorted and bobbed his head up and down, trying
to get the bit between his teeth so he could run
home. "No running on slippery cobbles, sir," Quill
told him sternly.

He knew once he reached his lane that Rutledge had preceded him. Half the staff was on the

steps, some crying, some wringing their hands. He drew up in front and handed Brutus's reins over to John, who was standing in the cold rain looking morose.

At that point a third carriage spun up to the house and stopped. He watched as Anna Kate hopped out, a young woman carrying a basket of food right behind her.

"What is it?" Anna called, alarm on her face.

"Rutledge," Quill said. "He found her."

Anna's face fell. She ran to Quill and threw herself into his arms. He thankfully wrapped his arms around her compact little body; it felt so warm, so alive. He buried his face in her hair, which smelled of jasmine.

"Oh, Quill," she said, once she could speak, "what will happen to her?"

He shrugged. "The worst. He will have her jailed now." One arm around her shoulders, which were shaking now with her sobs, he ascended the stairs.

"Quill," Anna said, "I have to tell you—Mme Vero, the milliner, came by. Someone—two men—traced Mr. Sumner to his house and beat him nearly to death, all to get Diana's name. It has to be Rutledge and his men."

"But how...? No, I know how, and why. We'll take care of that beast."

Quill approached his mother, standing in the door, looking bereft. "He's been? Did he hurt you?"

Schunk

Lady Wentworth shook her head, her face ravaged with grief. "I had left Lucas alone with Diana while I went to the kitchen to direct Cook about dinner. I went downstairs to check the wine cellar because Randall had told me one bottle of brandy had soured. The next I knew, there was a great commotion in the foyer. Randall was shouting for Mr. Lucas to come help him beat Rutledge off, but Lucas was out cold in Diana's room. Rutledge must have overpowered him from behind. He's been beaten about the face, I should imagine in payment for his good looks against Henry's evil countenance. Quill, she won't survive his treatment this time!"

He feared she was right. He ushered everyone back into the house. To the help he said, "You all need to get into dry clothes. We cannot cope with seven cases of pneumonia at this time. Mother, you look to be in shock. Anna, can you take Mother into the drawing room? Randall, bring them both some strong tea, with a dollop of brandy in it. And one for yourself too, man."

"Thank you, sir," Randall said. He bowed slightly at the earl. This was why he could tolerate the earl's sometime dark sullenness. He was invariably fair and considerate when the times called for it.

As everyone scattered, Quill stood still in the hall. He needed to take stock. He took a deep breath and ran one hand though his wet hair.

What to do next? Toby's planned dash to Kent

was now unnecessary. But he could use his friend's assistance while he tracked down Rutledge. He looked up the stairs. He should check on Lucas's condition. He sighed. Lucas's arrival was perhaps the trigger to this catastrophe, the one event Rutledge had hoped would lead him to Diana.

And the crusty old doctor perhaps dying from a beating by the Beast's men. He felt sick at heart. Diana's death seemed sure, one way or another, now or later.

He slowly went up the stairs to see Lucas. He heard Randall crossing the foyer below. "Randall," he called down, "Toby Esterby may arrive soon. Send him up to Diana's—" here he corrected himself— "to the ivory room, will you?"

"Yes, sir."

Lucas was standing at the window, watching the rain sluice down the glass. He didn't turn when Quill entered the room.

"I hear Henry did some damage to you," Quill said softly.

At first Lucas did not speak, did not move. "I will kill him," he said at last, turning to face Quill. His handsome face was cut and bruised from a savage beating. "I will find him and I will kill him." Quill saw tears start in the man's eyes before Lucas turned back to the window. "He followed me here. He laughed at me and said he knew the 'lovesick swain' would lead him to her. I will kill him, and then, if she is dead, I will kill myself."

CHAPTER 10

Anna Kate wished she could crawl into her own bed, under the comforters, and cry, scream to the heavens. Diana, darling Diana, was back in that monster's hands. Yet, she had to bring herself back to her present duty, caring for Quill's mother, who seemed to be in shock, her color a sickly gray. "Please sit here," Anna said kindly as she led the older woman to a satin chaise by the window.

Once Eleanor was seated, Anna knelt beside her and picked up her hands, which were cold as the rain beating against the window. She began to chafe the older woman's hands, to bring warmth back to them. She searched her mind for something of comfort to say, but she could find nothing.

Did Quill need comforting too, now that Diana was lost to him? She thought of his engulfing embrace earlier; it had felt like coming home after a long absence, but it was due to his feeling for Diana, not her.

Schunk

She heard his voice outside the door, then two other men's voices. He entered and crossed the room, a worried expression on his face. "How are you, Mother?" he asked gently. He placed his hand on Anna's shoulder. She tried not to move so he wouldn't decide she was the wrong person to touch. Now he looked at Anna closely, not absentmindedly as he had earlier in the day. "And you?"

She merely shook her head.

Eleanor took her hand out of Anna's to reach for her son. "I'll be fine, Quill. You must find her and bring her back."

He took a deep breath and held it. Anna watched his chest swell with the breath. "Yes, Mother. Toby is here to help, and Lucas is ready to join us."

"How is Lucas?" Even though she was ill, Eleanor thought of him.

"He will do. His rage at the moment will serve him well. It's later we must worry about him. We're off. I am certain Rutledge will take her straight to Newgate. We'll try to stop the proceedings, but I'm sure the judge will ignore me."

"Surely not," Eleanor protested. "If the judge is someone your father knew, you can press a claim against Rutledge."

Quill nodded, then leaned over to kiss his mother's cheek. He was so close, Anna could smell again his bay rum after-shave. She closed her eyes briefly to enjoy the moment. Then quickly he'd straightened and was gone.

"Wait!" she said to the closing door. "Quill, wait."

He turned on his heel when she came out of the drawing room. "May I go with you to New-gate?" He scowled and began to shake his head no. She reached up to touch his lips to stop him from speaking. "I'll follow in the carriage. Diana may need a woman to help her, if she continues as weak as she was earlier. I brought her some of the beef soup Cook Jemima used to make at Diana's grandmother's when we were young. Perhaps she will take some of it for strength."

Toby joined them at that moment, his homely face drawn and pale.

Still Quill stood scowling at Anna Kate's suggestion. She knew he meant to say no, but instead, when Toby said, "She makes sense, man," he nodded.

"This may be the worst decision I have ever made, but yes, you may go. We'll not wait for the carriage, so you'll have to get there on your own." With that he tossed his cloak, still smelling of the earlier rain, around his shoulders. "You have a maid with you?"

"Yes."

"We will go to the Old Bailey first, of course. He will have taken her there for a hearing. Tell my mother. I must run on."

She beamed at him to express her gratitude. He

seemed to do a double take, gazing at her smile, then he was gone.

Taking her leave from Lady Wentworth, who was now able to sit up and whose color had improved, she promised, "I'll be back as soon as I can to tell you anything we learn."

Eleanor reached for her hand and kissed it. "Thank you, my dear. You're a comfort to me."

The drive along Oxford Street to the Old Bailey seemed dreadfully long. Anna Kate wished she were on horseback too, so she could travel closer to Quill. She kept praying for Diana as the carriage hurtled along as fast as it could in the traffic.

It was near dusk, and the lamplighters were out. The lengthening shadows made Newgate Prison look even more sinister than she might have imagined. Rain and mud hindered her descent from the carriage, and the walk past the old, musty stone building, with the basket full of jars of soup on her arm, was very slippery. Poorly dressed people had lined up along the cobblestones in front of the prison, and Anna felt the misery engraved on their faces. They had no well-to-do, titled champion to help them, so their hopelessness was beyond her understanding. She ached for them.

John, Quill's coachman, stood across the street from the throng in front of the Old Bailey holding three horses as well as the ones with Quill's landau. He nodded slightly to acknowledge her presence.

Seeing the landau there raised Anna's spirits, confident Quill would rescue Diana and take her home.

She entered the court building with a shiver. Travis was close on her heels. "This place is horrific," she whispered to the young seamstress, who merely nodded.

The courtroom smelled of wet wool and unwashed bodies. Anna fumbled in her reticule for a scented handkerchief to cover the odors. Once she and Travis found a seat near the back, she looked for Quill, and for Diana and Rutledge as well. As she searched, she noticed how many shades of gray and drab the old clothing the crowd wore had faded into. It was as though once the fine garments had left their original owners' backs, they tripped headlong back to their natural earth tones, the browns and grays of the original fibers. The lack of color was depressing; she wished she could find an impoverished family with young girls she could dress in jewel-toned blues and reds and greens. Perhaps when Diana's crisis was over, she would.

At last she found Quill's dark head. She wished she could sit near him, but there was such a press of people, she could not reach him. She wondered how he had made his way through the mob, but then she knew others would as a normal course make room for him.

Schunk

Not four rows ahead, she saw Diana's wheat-blond head, bowed, Anna imagined, so no one could see her face. Anna's heart went out to her. So ill, so much in pain, so frightened.

They sat through three other cases, then Rutledge stood to signal to his solicitor to join him at the front of the courtroom. The low murmur of voices ceased when he stood; the people in the court could see this would be a case involving the nobility, and they were vitally interested in seeing how justice would play out for the rich and titled.

When Diana was led, nearly dragged, to the box by a large bailiff, a gasp went round the room. Somehow Rutledge had dressed her again in an old cotton wash dress, so she looked like someone of the lowest class. Anna heard people's whispers. Most had decided Diana was not of the Quality because of her ragged appearance. As a result she would summarily be found guilty.

Surely they could see the proud set of her head, the nobility of her carriage, as beaten as she was!

George Lyons, Rutledge's solicitor, made a slight bow to the judge, a red-faced, portly man who looked almost distinguished under his large white wig. "Your honor," he said, his stentorian tones ringing through the room, "my client befriended this young woman two years ago when she was thrown out of the house where she worked"—at that Anna gasped and struggled to rise, but the crowd surrounding her was straining forward, in front of her and around her, and she could not move— "and married her, out of the goodness of his heart."

At that a look of derision crossed Diana's face, and she straightened her back. Anna wanted to cheer her.

"Now she has stolen his family's jewels and run off to London to make her fortune."

Anna heard a snort and guessed it was Quill's.

"He desires that you charge her with robbery. He feels that the kindest thing to do for the wench would be to transport her so she cannot prey on good-hearted Englishmen such as he any longer." He paused, then gestured toward Diana in the box. "As you can see, if she were cleaned up, she would look quite beautiful. Her beauty deceived him and made him think she was also good."

At that point Rutledge rose and cleared his throat. "If I may, your honor, I must corroborate everything Mr. Lyons has said. I regret my own foolishness in marrying such a one, but I ask the court to remove her from our fair land so no one else may fall into her snare."

The crowd muttered its approval of his sentiment. Anna wondered how long this nonsense would go on. Again she tried to rise but could not. A large, fat woman, garlic on her breath, was leaning across her to see what was going on. Couldn't Quill at least stand and speak?

The crowd was beginning to call for a decision on her guilt. Their murmurings were rising, and disorder was growing.

The judge looked exasperated. He lifted his gavel and slammed it down. "Quiet, or I will have you all removed from the court. I will not tolerate this disorderliness. I will make my judgment on my own, without your help."

He sounded drunk, his words slurred. What kind of judge was he? An inebriated one, at least.

Again he raised his gavel. Surely he hadn't decided so soon? It couldn't be! This was a travesty. Diana hadn't even been allowed to speak in her own behalf.

"Your honor."

It was Quill! Anna wanted to shout with joy, but knew she must keep silent.

"Yes, Lord Wentworth."

"Lord Whitehead, may I speak?"

"Surely."

Quill made his way through the bodies blocking his route to the front of the room. Anna caught a glimpse of Rutledge's face as he watched Quill approach the bench. If ever a man hated another, Henry Rutledge hated Quillen Rossiter.

Quill turned to Henry and bowed slightly. "Mr. Rutledge," he said, with heavy emphasis on the "Mister." Then he turned back to Lord Whitehead. "Your honor, the facts of this matter are somewhat different from what Mr. Rutledge and his solicitor have stated. In fact, this young lady is just that, a lady. She is the granddaughter of Guy Windesor, the earl of Bruxton, and inherited his considerable wealth two years ago. Rutledge pursued her and deceived her, taking her away from Andover just hours before she was to wed Lucas Cranford, baron of Breckin."

Now the crowd was really grumbling. The fat woman next to Anna said, "The tide has turned, and we will not see a guilty verdict for this case." Her educated tone surprised Anna. "But maybe the plaintiff will be the next defendant. That may prove interesting."

"He told her that Lucas had been murdered on his way to the wedding and that the murderers were on their way to kill her too, in a vendetta against the Cranfords. He would keep her safe, but she must come quietly. Because he'd been a friend of her family's some time before, she believed him; in shock, she went with him."

Diana's head was still high, and her eyes, fixed on the distance, glimmered with tears.

"Rutledge had gotten a special license. He took her to Gretna Green and wed her there. Then, in the past twenty months, he has gone through her considerable estate, spending it all on women and gambling."

At that Rutledge took a step toward Quill, hands clenched before him. His solicitor placed a hand on Henry's chest, and he fell back.

"Diana Atwood Rutledge still has a small inheritance from her grandmother, in her name alone.

When she refused to hand it over to Rutledge, he began a full-scale physical assault on her. The marks on her neck, the wound that has re-opened in her side, are the result of the beating he gave two weeks ago. She ran away to find help, when she realized his plan was to accuse her of theft, of her own family's jewels. I have been keeping her at my home, under my mother's care, since."

The judge nodded, graciously. "Remember me to your lovely mother."

Henry's solicitor erupted, his face red. "I demand a new trial, with an impartial judge!"

The judge snarled at him. "Siddown before I have you removed from the court. How dare you question my judgment? I won't have it! I'll have you thrown in irons if you repeat such a statement! Do you understand?"

The solicitor nodded, somewhat subdued.

Once the crowd's murmurings had died down, Quill continued. "I ask you to release Diana Atwood Rutledge to my care until the facts of the matter can be made known. At this point it is only my word against Rutledge's."

This time the murmurings were in approval of Quill's statement. Anna could see he would do well in the Lords.

"What is the value of the missing jewels?" the judge asked Rutledge's solicitor.

After a brief consultation, the solicitor said, "Fifty thousand pounds, your honor."

Diana laughed. "Perhaps fifteen thousand pounds' worth remain, your honor. He has pawned or lost all of the others."

"Her word against mine," Henry shouted. "She's a born liar!"

"Quiet!" the judge thundered.

Still Anna could not rise. The heat of the warm bodies in the room was beginning to make her feel faint.

"Fifteen thousand pounds is quite a large sum," the judge said. "I will keep this woman over for further examination of the facts. You may find lodgings for her close to the prison, in case she is of the Quality. The conditions here would not suit a lady. But I won't allow her to go free until I have assurance that she is indeed what you say, Lord Wentworth. Are you championing her because you plan to marry her yourself, Wentworth? I can't recommend it—such a notorious female would be bad for your reputation."

"First, she is not notorious, except in that she is involved with a rotter like Rutledge. And no, I will not marry her, but I would like someone to, like this gentleman here,"—he pointed to Lucas— "if it will save her from that swine Rutledge, who is called the Beast by all who know him."

Rutledge threw himself across the small gap dividing him from Quill. He grabbed Quill by the throat and began throttling him. "I'll kill you for this, Wentworth!"

"Bailiff, subdue this man!"

By now the crowd was in an uproar. Nothing like a good fight among the Quality to spur on a crowd's bloodlust.

He banged his gavel down forcefully. "Silence," Judge Whitehead bellowed. "I will not have this disorder! Clear the courtroom."

At that point Anna grabbed Travis' hand. "Stay seated," she hissed, "when the court is cleared. Perhaps then we can speak."

Travis, big doe eyes wide, nodded. "This is dreadful," she whispered.

Precipitately, the crowd surged and swelled, then cleared around Anna and Travis. Anna pulled Travis to her feet. "Bring the basket!" Then she dragged Travis with her to stand against the inside wall of the courtroom, away from the exit.

At last the court had cleared, except for the judge, Quill, Lucas, Toby, and Diana. Rutledge had been removed to chambers, his solicitor with him.

Whitehead looked down on the four right in front of him, then back at the two young women huddled against the wall. "Well," he thundered, "what are you doing in here?" He pointed his finger at Anna and Travis. Anna could feel Travis quivering from fright.

"Your honor," Anna said, her voice sounding slight and squeaky in the empty room.

"Yes?" When Anna hesitated, he yelled, "What is it?"

"Your honor," she repeated, now making her way to the front of the room, holding on to Travis with one hand, Travis holding on to the basket. "My name is Anna Kate Forsythe. I'm from Diana Atwood's village, where my father is vicar. May I speak to her character, sir?"

"How do I know your father is a vicar, or even if so, not a blackguard?"

She gasped and pulled herself up straight. "My father a blackguard? Never! How dare...?"

"Anna," Quill cautioned quietly.

Anna noticed Diana had paled and now was leaning against the front of the dock. She feared Diana would faint, so she began to speak quickly.

"I beg your pardon, your honor. I am speaking the truth, and my father is the soul of virtue, sir. And Diana is my dearest friend, and she has been grievously mistreated by that wicked man, Henry Rutledge." Anna felt tears rise in her throat, then her eyes, but she was so angry she could not stop them. "She has been near death for the past few days, your honor. I have brought her some of her grandmother's cook's best beef soup, so she will eat and get her strength back. See, she is near fainting, sir. Please let us feed her and take her back to Lord Wentworth's home. His mother is worried sick over us all. We are none of us used to being brought before the court. Your honor."

A smile flitted across the judge's face, then he reached down below the bench for a flask. He tipped it up to drink, but it was obviously empty. He even shook it to make sure. "Well. It has been a long day. I will release this woman into your keeping, Lord Wentworth, but bring her back in two weeks. And at least three more witnesses as to her identity."

At that Lucas stepped forward, his jaw thrust forward. Anna hoped he would not offend the judge. "You already have three witnesses here," he stated aggressively. "I know her from childhood on, as does Quill, and as does Toby Esterby here. Miss Forsythe has spoken for her. What more do you need, man? She's been nearly killed."

The judge's face seemed to close at Lucas's words. "Young man, if Rutledge is her husband, he has the right to her property. If she has run away, he has the right to sue for her return."

Quill cleared his throat. "I apologize for our persistence, Lord Whitehead, but Rutledge does not want her back. He wants her transported to Australia. She will surely die on the ship, or find death in exile. Look at her!" Diana's eyes were closed, her face so white that she was surely near death. "She has done nothing wrong, except not to die from his beatings. I beg of you, sir, release her."

"Hear, hear," Toby said, then added, "your honor."

The judge stood and waved them wearily away. "Have her back in two weeks with signed statements as to the veracity of your claim about her identity.

Death in Exile

Do not fail, or to the prison ship she will go." With that he stomped from the room.

CHAPTER 11

Eleanor had recovered from her shock by the time the group returned to Wentworth Place. She had taken her heart medication, then ordered a large supper for them, with three meats, more of the soup Anna had prescribed for Diana, a heavy golden bread, a round of Stilton, and an apple cobbler with fresh cream.

Diana was back safe in the ivory room, asleep.

After they had eaten and were still sitting at the large mahogany table, Anna Kate wanted to throw herself on Quill's neck, she wanted to dance around the Wentworths' dinner table, she wanted to kiss everyone present. "Such a victory!" she said. "We even got Diana to eat some of that beef broth. She remembered how she loved it so when she was young and in her grandmother's care!"

No one answered. She looked around the table. No one else looked as jubilant as she felt.

Quill spoke. "It isn't over yet, Anna."

Toby shook his head. "He's right, you know. There's a long road ahead of her, of us all."

Lucas merely continued to stare at the table before him, fiddling with his silver. Anna was beginning to worry about him and his long silences, his anger. But Diana was going to get well and then perhaps get a divorce from that rat Rutledge and be able to marry Lucas, who could then get back to normal.

Anna tossed back her head. "But the worst part is over, I know it is." The three men stared at her, but she went on. "Now that Diana is eating, she will begin to mend. And what can Rutledge do, now that the judge knows something is amiss?"

Lucas stood abruptly, knocking his chair over against the wall behind him. "Little Miss Sunshine. You always were a perennial optimist. Don't you understand the implacable hatred of a man bested and shamed before other men? He will not quit now. We all must watch our backs."

The deep growl of bitterness in his voice gave Anna Kate the shivers. "I...I'm sorry, Lucas," she said, head lowered. "Of course you're right."

He pivoted on his heel and left the room.

She turned to Lady Wentworth. "I apologize for oversetting your guest, my lady."

Lady Wentworth nodded graciously. "He has overset himself. This is very painful for him."

"Thank you for your kindness to me. I must be going back to the Stanfields. I have been remiss in my duties to them. Constance is so good to me that I must not take advantage."

When she stood up, Quill and Toby did also.

"I will call your carriage," Quill said. "And the little Travis. I imagine this has been a long day for her too."

"Yes, milord—I mean, Quill. Thank you."

The rain had passed, and the moon and stars sparkled an icy, brittle light in the frigid night air. Travis yawned widely from her seat across from Anna in the carriage. "I have kept you out so late," Anna said, apology in her voice.

"But it has been gratifying. Rarely does one see so many different kinds of people or so many different emotions in one place as that courtroom. It was so different from the last time we were there." Travis caught herself, then bit her lip.

"The last time?"

Tears sprang to her eyes. "Oh, I shouldn't be telling you this. Lady Stanfield knows, of course."

"Knows what?" Anna asked gently, afraid of frightening the young woman to silence.

"My father. He was had up before a judge there two years ago. He had been arrested with a snare in his possession. The squire of the farm where we lived accused him of trapping animals on his property. The warden on the farm told him he could snare rabbits for supper. The warden had even given him the snare."

"And then what happened?" Anna knew the

gentry could have access to all the game on their own property, and their tenants could not touch a hair on even a rabbit's foot.

"The squire and the warden testified against him. The warden of course lied. Papa was sentenced to transportation to Australia for seven years, but he died there soon after his arrival. We were all, my mother and my five younger brothers and sisters, thrown on the county's care. Lady Stanfield—Constance—learned of it from her cousin, the squire's wife, and tried to redeem us all. My mother died of heartbreak soon after. She had been suffering from consumption for some time, and we knew her time would end soon. My brothers have gone to sea as sailors and my baby sister is in Reading at school. Lady Constance has been very good to us."

Anna marveled at her calm. "I am so sorry."

Travis patted her hand. "I hold no bitterness. What happened can't be changed. But today was heartening, to see people like you and Lord Wentworth stand up for a falsely accused person."

"It was heartening," Anna Kate said, "only because Diana was released to his lordship's care. It could have gone so badly for her, as it did for your father. I was right to feel near frightened to death."

"But you sounded so brave and bold when you stood up to the judge."

"Oh, dear, don't tell me that. Quill despises the bold, brazen thing I can be at times."

Travis looked at her a long moment. "Oh, Miss

Anna, I do not believe that is so. He likes you just fine."

Anna blushed. She was glad for the dark in the carriage, so Travis could not see her emotions on her face. "You are kind to say so," she said quietly. "What is your given name?"

"Susan."

"I'll call you that. You make a good friend."

The drive home lulled Anna into a heavy-headed doze, and once the carriage stopped in front of the Stanfields, a weight of depression fell over her like a heavy woolen cloak. She felt she could hardly walk up the stairs into the house, and she still had three more flights to go to reach her room. Her room where she lived as a servant.

During her time this evening with the Wentworths, she had forgotten her place and fallen in with the general air of belonging with the *ton*. She did not belong with lords and ladies, and while Quill had been kind to her today, he knew she did not.

He had told the judge he did not plan to wed Diana; that had encouraged Anna at the time. But she knew, as well as she knew her own name, that he would not marry her either.

Anna Kate slept late the next morning. When she awoke to hear her clock chime eleven, she jumped out of bed, ashamed of how she was failing at her position.

She felt the cold seeping in around the large window on the west side of her room, so she dressed hurriedly in a heavy blue coach dress with red piping. Giving the most perfunctory of brushings to her hair, she checked on the safety of Diana's black velvet pouch in her wardrobe, then hurried downstairs to the kitchen, where she hoped to find some small breakfast.

Cook smiled when Anna entered the vast, stone-flagged kitchen. The room was warm and smelled of cinnamon and sugar, and warm yeast breads.

"I am sorry to be so late for breakfast, Cook. May I serve myself a small portion of something, anything? And may I get myself a cup of coffee?"

Cook flapped her apron at her. "Ye need to be gettin' yer beauty rest if yer to go to Almack's. Yer face is white as a sheet, and those circles! We expected ye to sleep later than this. Get yerself to the morning room. I will send ye a meal on a tray. The Lady would have me neck if I fed ye in the kitchen. Ye're on the marriage track now, and no longer belowstairs, me miss. Out ye go."

Anna obeyed, but she felt confused. She remembered, belatedly, the conversation she'd had days before with Aunt Lydia. She had given Anna three days to wind up her duties with the children, and now those days of being in charge of Mary and Paul were over. She felt a pang.

Constance entered the morning room soon after Anna herself, a sweet smile on her face. "Good morning, dear heart. I thought surely you would sleep past noon."

Anna felt herself flush. "I...I fear I have failed the children."

"Nonsense. Of course you haven't. Their grandmother is glad of an excuse to spend all her time with them, now that she knows Lady Wentworth has taken up your *parti*. Today she has taken them to the museum." Constance served her a cup of coffee. "Lady Wentworth has sent a message to you. Diana is some better—" At this Anna gasped in relief. She could have wagered the disastrous outing of the day before would have set Diana back. "They have planned to move her out of town, for they fear Rutledge will try again to abduct her."

Mrs. Godwin entered with a tray for Anna, with kippers, bacon, fluffy yellow eggs scrambled high on the plate, and a dish of prunes and apricots next to the plate. "Oh! I will never be able to eat so much! I must hurry to Wentworth Place to see Diana before she leaves."

"That is the other part of the message. Quill asks that you not come now. Wait until he is gone with her."

Anna felt as though she'd had the carpet yanked out from under her. He was denying her the pleasure of seeing either one of them. "But—why?"

Schunk

"So Rutledge will know you have no knowledge of where she is. And you are to stay in, until he gets back to town, unless you are in the care of two menservants, he said. He is worried about your safety." Constance said the last very gently, as though trying to persuade Anna of its truth.

A rush of anger stiffened her back. "I have to stay in? All the time?"

"Yes. Besides, you will be kept too busy in the next few days to go out anyway. Mother Stanfield has ordered Madame Vero to come and bring samples of fabrics. She is ordering you five new dresses for the Season. And you will be going to Almack's in a little over two weeks."

"Almack's? I don't want to go to Almack's! I'm sure I would feel like a slab of meat on a hook at such a place. And Quill would hate me forever if I go there. He does not like frivolous female behavior."

"Quill is the one who got you an invitation. He has asked Sir Toby to take you. He cannot go himself."

With that Anna's heart fell. She really had not believed Quill would take her, she knew he would never do such a thing, but to know he had palmed her off on Toby! "I think I may die of humiliation," she said. She stood slowly, to be sure to behave decorously. "Please excuse me. I must go to my room."

Sadly, with heavy heart, she climbed the stairs to her room. No more Diana to see, and no more

Death in Exile

Quill.

Once she reached her room, she wandered aimlessly about, touching first one thing and then another, the drapes, the ewer on the washstand, the blue gauze of the angel tester. She felt like a bird in a gilded cage, a very small, blue bird in a very large, very opulent cage. What was to become of her? She was to be auctioned off in the marriage mart, and there was only one buyer she had a taste for, only one, who had won her heart many years before.

Chapter 12

The next few days passed so slowly. At times Anna Kate thought she would scream. The selection of dress patterns having already been supervised by Mme Vero, her assistant came on the Wednesday, bringing with her some gorgeous fabrics, in rose, blue, and a lovely self-striped white silk for her appearance at Court. She could have enjoyed the prospects of lovely new frocks if only she could see Diana and, yes, Quill again.

How much she longed to see his face surprised her. She castigated herself for a moonstruck calf.

Mme Vero herself came late Wednesday, and Anna Kate had an opportunity to ask her about Mr. Sumner.

Tears glittered in Madame's eyes as she said, "He's still not speaking. The doctor fears permanent damage to his brain, from the beating."

"I'm so sorry. I wish there were something I could do."

Mme Vero shook her head. "Thank you, but there is nothing, but perhaps prayer." She raised her head. "What about the young woman the Beast was looking for? How is she now?"

"I don't know. She is sequestered someplace, and I don't even know where."

On Thursday she had a long letter from her father, and he hadn't even bothered to write crosswise the pages; she'd never known him to be so profligate, using six sheets of paper.

He told her how much he missed her, and how much he had been looking forward to her visit home at Christmas. "But now," he wrote, "I understand that is a pleasure I must forego. Your aunt Stanfield wrote in profuse apology about forgetting to give you a Season. But of course I am the one who was remiss. I was not ready to see my dear Anna Katherine a young lady already. And of course, I had not thought of a Season for you, although now I am powerless to understand why I did not."

She could not go home for Christmas! But she had been looking forward to it so much. She felt stifled in London, now that Aunt Lydia had decided she was to be a lady. Drat! She knew Aunt Lydia would not swerve from her course, and because of that, Papa would not give in, even if she begged for hours.

She went back to the letter. "Of course it is because I do not want to give you up. Once you marry, you will no longer be my little Anna, but I do not want you to go through life alone. I will not be here forever."

That sentiment sent chills down her back. The thought of Papa dying some day? She supposed she realized it was a possibility, but not any time soon.

She pictured her father in her mind, his hair white now, his blue eyes pale and mild, his manner kind and courteous. He had always been rake thin, but hearty enough. She could not remember a day of illness for him over the years.

She best remembered his long, thin fingers holding a book. He read nearly all the time. He had studied at Oxford and taken a first in classical languages. A very bright man, her father, and with it too gentle to compete in the business world. And he loved music. When she sat at the piano in the music room to play, he always gravitated to the settee in the bow window near her to listen. He loved Bach.

A Boxing Day, three years ago now, she thought, sprang to her mind. Quill had been there, in the vicarage with her as she played for her father.

Papa had been grieving over the death of his brother, Kenneth Forsythe, organist at Winchester. They had been close and had shared a love of Bach. She began to play "Toccata and Fugue in D Minor" when Quill came up behind her to tease her, perhaps, she'd hoped, to kiss her hair. She heard her father's step, and to keep her father from walking in on a romantic scene, had stopped him with a short, "Not now, Quill."

She remembered he'd inhaled so vigorously that her hair had moved in the breeze. Then, after that, he stayed only briefly to speak to her father, then left abruptly. The next thing she knew, she heard that he had gone up to London to stay.

Anna Kate had never understood what had happened that day. She had been hoping he would pay her court, but he never came back.

A large part of the problem was the clash of personality between them, he so serious, she too light-brained in his estimation. Her heart ached now at what she had lost. She took out a clean sheet of paper and began to trace his name, over and over. He'd been a true friend, one she had felt she could spend her life with, besides being breathtakingly handsome and charming.

Well, maybe not so charming, she thought, remembering his black rage of a week ago. Debonair and dashing, though—those two terms she could attest to.

She crumpled up the paper and threw it away.

Anna Kate stared at the paper in the waste can, then retrieved it. After smoothing it out, she began to make a list on the back of it of the odd occurrences. She tried to remember the sightings of the strangers, here and at Quill's, and she wrote down the approximate times for their spying. She thought and thought but could make no sense of it. She just didn't have enough facts to make a case.

Death in Exile

Perhaps if she went to the Two Swans. She'd heard Lucas, Toby, and Quill talking about seeing the men there, at least the round-faced man with the bushy black beard.

Constance and Aunt Lydia would have a conniption if they knew she was plotting this. Yet what else could she do that would make a difference? Sitting here on silk and satin upholstery sure wouldn't help anyone catch Rutledge.

She corrected herself: not that she hoped to catch him herself, in the flesh, at least. What could she do with him?

She quickly made a perusal of her wardrobe; the only things that looked like inconspicuous attire was an olive green riding habit. It was old and not at all dashing, so she wouldn't draw attention to herself. And she would put her hair up and wear a hat and veil. A veil, inconspicuous? Maybe not. A half-veil, the charcoal gray one that fit her riding hat. And she'd keep her head down, her eyes cast on the ground, not look in a fresh, challenging fashion into people's faces.

Anna Kate remembered how to saddle a horse from childhood, so she didn't need the help of the stableman. And this was a good time to go, with perhaps the man snatching a postprandial nap in the back of the stable.

Once she'd changed and sneaked out of the house, she got to the stable to find things weren't as easy as she'd hoped. Only the little pony mare belonging to the children was there; all the other horses were gone.

"Drat!" she said. "Wouldn't you know...?" There was no saddle for the mare in plain sight. Did she have to rig up the pony cart and drive it? It was done at home in the village; Miss Merrill, the town spinster, did it all the time. Could she pretend she was another Miss Merrill? It looked as if she would end up a spinster, so why not?

With some struggles, including tearing her nails and having her hair come straggling down, Anna Kate succeeded in getting the pony harnessed in the cart and out of the stable before she was discovered. What would the stableman think if he got back before she did? That the pony and cart had been stolen? No, surely not. He'd think someone had taken the children out for a spin.

She drove the cart on quiet side streets as much as she could, in order to avoid undue attention. She made a wrong turning just before the Two Swans but corrected it easily and ended up coming at it from the opposite, farther side, which didn't matter for her purposes. In fact, it was a serendipitous mishap, for Rutledge stood in front of the inn now, his back to her as he argued with two men, one the round-faced man with the bushy black beard, the other the tall, slim man she'd seen the once, at Quill's in Mayfair.

Three such distinct types made unlikely cohorts. Why was the slim, elegant man hanging about with such as the Beast and the ordinary bearded man? He didn't seem to match them, in attire or manner.

The elegant man began to speak, and Anna Kate edged the pony cart closer, in hopes of hearing his words. She looked, not at them, but toward the door of the inn, in hopes they'd think she was waiting for someone to come out of the inn.

"Here's that poor old woman's letter, Rutledge," he said.

"What woman?" Rutledge growled.

"The housekeeper you sent off without even a character reference. That wasn't smart of you. And she wrote your name in it."

"My name! Why?"

"To blame you, of course, for mistreating her and Lady Diana also. You've been unwise, Rutledge, and I'm trying to save your tail. You'd better pay up."

"Blackmail now?" he said with a sneer.

"No, just an added impetus to get you to pay your debts. I paid 100 pounds for it to the footpad who killed her; you can pay me all you owe me and I'll give it to you."

Rutledge grabbed him by the collar. "People are saying I killed her, and I didn't. But you know who did."

The slim, elegant man removed Rutledge's fat sausage fingers with obvious distaste. "Don't touch me," he said quietly but with an underlying fierceness. "I don't know his whereabouts; he made himself scarce."

At that point Anna Kate realized she was staring at the men, and that they had noticed her.

"Here, now, who's that woman watching us?" the bearded man asked, pointing at her.

She couldn't believe the sensation of pure fear, how it seemed to send an electric charge through her, how it made her heart leap into her throat. This was why some people fainted from fear.

Knowing she needed to seem oblivious to them, she dropped her eyes and turned the pony cart around, slowly as she could bear, deliberately, so they would not notice anything odd about her.

She hoped.

As she drove off, she felt their eyes boring into her back, but they didn't follow her.

His landau with Diana in it ahead of him, he on Brutus, Quill made the long journey to Kent in low spirits. He hugged his greatcoat closer around him. The rain had fallen steadily all morning, and the air was chill as a dungeon.

He re-thought the strategy they had adopted, with Toby going west to Hampshire, Lucas toward Brighton, the landau north for a few miles, he himself going due east. Then after one hour of travel they were all to change routes, go the opposite way, then switch once more, to head toward Kent. They made up this elaborate plan in hopes of fooling Rutledge, but what if it didn't work? Dire results for poor Diana, if it didn't.

Quill had just caught up with the landau not five miles up the road. Had they fooled Rutledge? He could not guess. The man was so driven with viciousness that he seemed capable of anything. He rode on, drowned in negative thoughts.

He remonstrated with himself, for he should be thankful Diana was doing so well. The pleasure of seeing Anna the day before, the victory in court over Rutledge—temporary as it might be—and then the nourishment she'd finally taken when Anna had brought the famous soup—all those factors had helped her begin to heal.

Anna really had done their friend a world of good. For that matter, she did him a world of good too, when she wasn't maddening him. He grinned at the thought of her spirit. She was strong and daring, besides being heartrendingly beautiful and intelligent to boot.   ·

His mother had doubted his interpretation of Anna's words those three long years ago. Had he misunderstood? Had she not been refusing his suit? Had his pride interfered with his understanding her motives? He didn't know, so he needed to talk to her and find out. He purposed to, once he returned to London. The time spent with her in the past week convinced him he had not put her out of his heart that Boxing Day, even if he had sworn to himself he had.

The sun was nearing its winter-weak zenith, and soon it would be time to stop for a small meal at the inn Toby had told him about at Dandridge.

Spurring Brutus on, he caught up to the landau. "John!" he shouted. "Pull up."

Once the carriage stopped, he swung down from the horse and dropped the reins so the beast could nibble the dry grasses along the road. He knocked softly on the door, then opened it. "Diana, how are you making the trip?"

The navy blue carriage dress she wore and the heavy camel-colored greatcoat Quill had lent her in London set off her delicate beauty. Her hair and skin were beginning to look healthy again. Still, she seemed weak. She smiled at him. "It's a rough ride, but I feel wonderful. So good to be out of his reach." She did not need to name whom she meant.

He reached in and patted her hand. "I know. Your color looks good."

She bowed her head slightly. "I feel quite well."

"We are nearly to the inn Toby specified for our dinner. Are you hungry?"

"Ravenous." She smiled broadly at him, then sobered. "But I am worried about Anna Kate. She will fret about us."

"I sent her a message."

"But with so few particulars. I must write her when we arrive, and you can carry my letter back with you. She has been so good to me."

He nodded. "You're right. She doesn't know how much good she's done you, and she will worry. But I could not tell her more, and I couldn't let her come along. You know she would have insisted on coming if I'd let her speak to me at all. She does have a bull-doggish manner when she wants something."

"I know. So dear of her."

"Let's hurry. I don't want to tarry on the road."

He mounted Brutus. Twirling about, the horse dashed off up the road to Dandridge. Quill imagined the creature knew there was a scoop of oats awaiting him just around the bend.

Just as he came up over the swell of hills before the small village, he noticed up ahead a shiny black carriage with three white plumes painted on the door. He reined his horse around and raced back to the landau. "Turn, John, turn," he said as distinctly as he could, without raising his voice. "He's beaten us here. But how?"

Diana stuck her head out the window. "Rutledge is here? No one could have told him." She gritted her teeth. "His father came from Kent. Could he be visiting kin?" She frowned as she thought. "He has a cousin somewhere around Tonbridge who is said to be as dissipated as he. Do you think he has come to find this cousin, to enlist his aid?"

Quill shrugged. "I can't guess. Who is this cousin?"

"Lyndel, Lord Basham. There's another younger cousin, too, somewhere around."

"Reinforcements. We have to turn around. The worst thing is, I can't get word to Toby and Lucas. They'll be along soon."

"Milord, if I may make a suggestion," John said.

"Yes?" Quill snapped.

"If you would entrust me with Brutus, you could drive the landau. Rutledge does not know me. I could go ahead to the inn and get some rations for the trip, then wait over in that copse"—he pointed toward a stand of beech trees— "until Toby and Lucas come. You go to Sevenoaks and wait. Sir," he added, as though fearful he had overstepped his bounds.

"Excellent idea. I don't think Brutus will play up too much for you."

"Oh, no, milord. I ride him two or three times a week to be sure he will take me."

At that Quill scowled. "What?"

"I apologize for taking the liberty, but I did not think he should be a one-man horse."

Quill snorted. "Well. Just as well, under the circumstances. Next time, though, you have such an independent notion, do clear it with me first."

"Yes, milord." John grinned his endearing grin and climbed down from the landau. "The horses are nearly blown, but they will get you to Sevenoaks."

"Thank you, John." Quill wasn't quite sure how

to deal with a coachman who was quite so resourceful. Should he be punished, or congratulated? For now, the question didn't matter; getting Diana to safety did. "Buy a round of cheese, plenty of bread, and some ale. We will need the sustenance," he said, throwing him a small purse of coins.

"Yes, milord." He tugged at his forelock and grinned mischievously.

"And no slip up. Take care he does not connect you to us." He frowned as the splendid horse and its handsome rider turned to head toward Dandridge. "Wait up, John. You had better tell that horse to play poor. He is entirely too handsome a piece of horseflesh."

John nodded, then nudged Brutus's left shoulder with the toe of his boot. "Play poor," he whispered, "so the bad man cannot guess what you are." At that Brutus began to limp, favoring his left hind leg, and collapsed his lungs in some odd way to look less virile.

CHAPTER 13

Time hung heavy on Anna Kate's hands, unused as she was to sitting and doing nothing. If she hadn't been so well brought up by her father, she would have thrown fits by now. Even the air inside the mansion seemed dull and stultifying.

She'd had letters from three of her old students at Andover. She needed to answer but could not force herself to concentrate.

She'd taken to running up and down the upper two flights of stairs—gingerly, to avoid notice—to conquer her need to scream or kick the walls. Somehow, her illicit trip to the Two Swans made her less patient, not more. She kept feeling she ought to do something, anything.

Late afternoon on Monday, at the end of the long, interminable days, Toby came to call. "He has brought a friend, Anna Kate," Constance said once she entered Anna's room where she was again reading her father's last letter, "a fellow soldier. They have some interesting tales to tell about soldiering."

Anna felt like shrugging, but controlled her ill-tempered impulse. "You find them interesting?"

"Why, yes. Don't you? But then again, I opine you do not know." Constance's face was glowing. "Sir Matthew Dunstable, Toby's friend, served briefly with Ansten in Canada. He saw him not two months ago, and brings me greetings from him. My most recent letters have not been getting through. When Matthew returns, he can take a pouch of letters with him, as well as new socks and gloves Mary and I knitted for him."

Anna rose and sighed. "New socks won't help with my situation with Quill."

"I know this time is hard for you. I pass the time waiting for Ansten with the children and with running the house. That helps. Perhaps you can find something of import to do and that will help you."

"Like rolling bandages, you think?" she snapped.

Constance recoiled; her face registered shock at Anna's comment.

Anna gasped and covered her mouth. "Oh, I'm so sorry. I've spoken out of my own selfishness and offended you. I didn't know… How I have such a penchant for opening my mouth and saying the wrong thing, I'll never know."

Constance's face was gray. "We each have our own pains and losses. Your longing for Quill is as trying to you as mine for Ansten. And yours may

be worse. You have nothing of his to keep you se-
cure in his love. But I believe it will come." With
that Constance kissed her husband's cousin on the
cheek and left her in her room.

The tears began to fall as Anna dealt with the
pain of her own failings, of missing Quill, of having injured her friend. "Will I ever grow past this
horrible place in my life, dear Lord? Will I ever be
strong and elegant and kind, like Constance and like
Diana?" She walked slowly, like an old woman, to
her bed where she lay down to cry for a few moments.

At last she arose and washed her face. She had
company awaiting her in the drawing room. If nothing else, she must present an interior calm and a
warm welcome to the two men who had come to
see her.

She entered the drawing room with some trepi-
dation. *What may I say to wound or goad this time?*
she asked herself. *I am thoroughly sick unto death of
myself.* She faced Toby and his friend as calmly as
she could.

Both men rose when she entered. "Good
evening," she said.

"Miss Forsythe." Sir Matthew bowed to her,
keeping his eyes on her.

He was quite handsome, she thought. Tall and
slim, with a noble head and perfectly draped neck
cloth, she recognized him at once as a young dandy.
He had abundant auburn hair and green eyes that

were examining her a mite too closely.

"Sir Matthew," she said, offering her hand to him, then to the other, "and Sir Toby. It is kind of you to call. Please, won't you be seated? May I offer you tea?"

"No, Anna, we cannot stay too long," Toby said formally as he strained to speak like the Quality; instead he ended up sounding stilted.

Still Sir Matthew kept his eyes boldly on her face. She was beginning to feel uneasy, as a pressure rose in her to say something caustic about it. She realized that that was a warning: she was tempted to correct him as she would any student in a classroom. She resolved to hold her tongue very firmly.

Toby cleared his throat. He flushed, then began to speak softly. Sir Matthew seemed not to listen, as taken as he seemed to be with Anna's appearance. "Anna, I come to bring you a message from Miss—your friend."

Anna stiffened. She turned her eyes to stare at Toby, her fingers tearing at her handkerchief.

"She is well and asks to be remembered to you."

Anna matched his soft tone. "How kind of you to bring me her news. When did you last see her?"

"Yesterday. She and her cousin arrived safely at their destination."

Anna smiled broadly, imagining herself to look a perfect ninny, to respond so strongly to a simple greeting. "Splendid. And did she say when they will return?"

"No, but not soon, is my opinion."

She glanced at Sir Matthew to see if he noticed anything strange about the message. Still he continued his overdone visual devouring of her face and form.

"And I have another message. Her cousin asked me to escort you to Almack's. I regret to say I cannot."

Anna returned her gaze to the tall, skinny redhaired man before her. "Oh?"

"No, I regret to say I'd already promised to escort a young lady, Miss Camilla Drayton-Day. But, by your leave, I have asked Dunstable here to make a foursome with us that evening. So in a way I will still escort you," he said, stumbling a bit in his embarrassment, "but so will he."

Still Sir Matthew continued to stare. Anna began to wonder if he was touched in the head. She shrugged a question at Toby, who seemed to understand her meaning: *who is he?* "He is quite a good friend of mine, and I can vouch for him."

Finally Dunstable seemed to awaken from his trance. "I do apologize, Miss Forsythe." His voice was deep and resonant. "You must find me a slow-top today. I suppose I have been too long away on the frontier. But your beauty quite overcomes my sense of propriety."

She blushed. "Once you speak, you do it charmingly. Thank you for the compliment."

"May I have the pleasure of accompanying you

to Almack's? I would be honored. And I promise not to stare that night. I will be quite recovered from my fit." He smiled then, and Anna was drawn in by the charm of his smile, the white teeth, the warm eyes.

"I would be delighted, Sir Matthew."

The rest of the visit passed quickly, once the men began regaling her with their war stories. They were so entertaining that she forgot her earlier bad temper and peevishness. After about an hour, they excused themselves, Matthew promising to return to visit her, if that met her fancy. She said, "That would be quite lovely."

Toby managed to get Matthew out the drawing room door before him, with a request to the butler to ask Lady Stanfield to have communications and gifts to Ansten ready by next midweek, then turned to whisper to Anna Kate: "They had a very close call with Rutledge."

Anna gasped. "No!"

"Yes, but Quill and his coachman, too, thought fast and escaped his notice."

She exhaled the breath she hadn't realized she was holding. "Thank God."

"They are fine, and they both miss you. Diana is finding her hosts quite entertaining. Quill will be sending a letter before long."

Tears sprang to her eyes. "Really?"

"Really." With that he leaned over and kissed her lightly on the cheek. "Try not to fret."

She dabbed at her eyes with her handkerchief. "I am becoming quite the watering pot these days." "I know. Quill is out of balance over you too." Her eyes widened. "Truthfully?"

"Truthfully, but he'll have my head if he learns I told you so." He mimed a worried stance, a hand on his heart, the other arm outstretched in mock supplication. "Please, dear lady, protect my guilty secret."

At that she giggled. "Oh, go on, you. I will not tell, never fear."

"I must leave. Dunstable will be getting suspicious. He is quite smitten with you. Someone needs to tell Quillen Rossiter that small fact. That will wake him up. He needs to claim you before someone else does."

She shook her head at him, but when the two men took their leave, her heart was lightened.

Constance joined her in the drawing room soon after.

Anna smiled shyly at her, then took her hand. "You were right, they were quite interesting." She lowered her gaze and pressed Constance's hand. "I don't know if you can ever forgive me for what I said earlier..."

"Of course I can forgive you. You were merely upset."

"You forgive only because of the goodness of your heart, not because it was forgivable. I will strive to control my tongue, and also my mood. I have no reason to moon about the place. I have nothing to carp about. You will detest me soon if I continue to act the infant while you remain so noble. I promise you I will try to emulate your example."

Constance's eyes softened. "Dear Anna, you are merely young. You will do fine as you grow."

"Thank you for your kind words, but I am truly too old to be wearing a Friday face all the time." She stretched on tiptoe to place a kiss on her friend's cheek. "Do you think I could read to the children after tea? I miss them, and Aunt Lydia has quite stolen them away from me. They are charming so I do not lay blame at her feet, but I would pray for some of their time also."

At that long formal speech, Constance laughed. "Of course, you may. I have been trying to spare you their chatter the past few days, but I see I did you an injustice. And they have missed you dreadfully." She put her hand gently on Anna's cheek. "Dear, funny Anna."

"Lord Wentworth, you look pensive."

Quill turned away from the window where he had been staring out at the rain. "Oh, forgive me, Miss Austen. I fear I am poor company." He walked over to the tea table where Cassandra Austen presided over potted meat sandwiches and petit fours. Diana and Jane Austen had already excused themselves from tea, Diana to rest and Jane to write, although she too claimed to be resting. Outside the family she was still secretive about her writing, Cassandra had told him several days earlier. He went on, "Would you mind if I were to leave Diana here with you for a few days?"

"Not at all," she assured him. She had a lovely speaking voice, as did her sister.

"I feel I need to get back to London for a time. Yet I fear leaving her in case Rutledge hears of her whereabouts and pursues her here, putting you in jeopardy."

"Oh, pooh!" she said, then looked abashed. "That sounded vulgar. Please forget I said such a thing. We will be in no danger. Two of our brothers are here for a stay, and they are big strong types. Besides, my brother Edward Knight has enough servants around to keep us safe." She smiled sheepishly at him. "And on top of that, my sister loves the intrigue. She says it is grist for her new novel."

He picked up a petit four and straightened, putting it into his mouth rather ceremoniously. Once he'd eaten it, he dusted off his hands and spoke. "I do appreciate your hospitality. My mother assured me you and Miss Jane Austen had a soul of warm welcome. I'll tell her she was right. I will take my leave now."

"So late in the day? Surely you can wait until morning."

"No," he said, with a gesture toward the window facing west. "I fear a winter storm is moving in. I must make as much speed today as possible. I'll stay at some inn along the way."

"But not at Dandridge, I avow."

"No, not at Dandridge. I do not wish to run into that rotter Rutledge again." He sketched a quick bow and left her.

Once Quill had left, Cassandra went in search of her sister. "He has gone back to London. I fear we have been witnesses to a man deeply in love."

Jane sighed. "It does not look quite so silly on him as it tends to on young females. He is quite dashing." She picked up a piece of paper from her desk. "That funny little royal librarian Mr. Clarke has written again. It was not enough for him that I acquiesced in dedicating *Emma* last year to that odious Prince he works for. He persists in this notion that I write a story about a humble but terribly important parson."

"Like him, I suppose," Cassandra said with a laugh.

Jane joined her in laughter. "Yes, I am sure precisely like him. I fear my gentle refusals have not penetrated his thick hide. I shall have to be blunt, to discourage his attentions."

"Oh, Jane, do you believe he is in love with you?"

"He is in love with himself and would be gratified to have me on his arm. Although why a man
would want as poor a specimen as I, I do not know."

"He knows Prinny thinks highly of you. Just
imagine the coup it would be for him to claim you
as his wife. Prinny would be green with envy."

"At least the Prince cannot pursue me as a wife,
although I suppose he might think he could set me
up in some small jewel of a house in St. James.
Dratted man, even if he is Regent. He is cruel to his
wife, and he would be cruel to a different one, or to
a paramour." She turned longingly back to the
manuscript she was fair-copying.

"You want to get back to work. I'll go look in
on Diana, then order the meals for tomorrow."
Cassandra kissed her sister on the cheek and took
her leave.

Not long after Cassandra had ordered the meals,
she began a new self-assigned task, to air the linen
cupboards. Before she'd made a good start at it, the
butler interrupted her.

"There's a visitor, Miss."

"Who is it?"

"Lyndel, Lord Basham."

"I don't believe I know him. Does Edward?"

"Slightly, Miss," he said in a cool tone that told
Cassandra that Lord Basham was not highly re-
garded by Edward Knight.

"What does he want?"

"I do not know, Miss."

Schunk

She sighed and pushed flyaway hair back into her bun. "Ask him to wait, please. I'll be there in a moment."

She didn't rush to neaten up for the man. She merely wanted to make sure her face was clean; her hands certainly felt dusty. At last, however, she entered the room to see a tall, well-dressed man standing at the window and looking out at the gray, angry lake beyond the house. The storm was moving in.

She offered her hand. "Lord Basham?"

He crossed the room to take her hand and bowed low over it. "Miss Austen. I'm pleased to make your acquaintance. You surely wonder why I'm here."

The man had a long, thin face and an aristocratic bearing, with fine bone structure, down to his well-kept hands. His manners were impeccable, and his face sincere.

"Please have a seat and tell me your errand."

"I'm looking for a relative of mine, and I wondered if you'd seen her lately. I understand she's a friend of yours."

"Yes?"

"Jane Rutledge; surely you know her."

Cassandra froze. Why would this man ask her about Diana? No one would have any reason to believe they knew each other! "Whom did you say? I didn't catch…"

"Diana Jane Atwood, she was, now Rutledge."

Death in Exile

What a situation to be in. He seemed upright and sincere, but she knew Diana's whereabouts were to be kept secret. What to do? "No, I'm sorry," she said, reluctant to lie, but unable to give the poor woman away, "I don't recall the name. What connections does she have? How would I know her?"

"She's a cousin of mine. I'd heard she was sick and that you were a nurse par excellence. My contacts in the area told me she'd surely be with you if not well."

Cassandra shook her head. "No, I'm sorry, someone has overvalued my abilities, and I can't help you. I'm here only for a visit with my brother for a time."

His face fell.

Again Cassandra felt he was sincere in his concern for his cousin. "May I offer you some tea? The weather threatens to get nasty, and perhaps you need some sustenance for your travel?"

He smiled, his face drawn. "It's very kind of you, but I must continue to look for her. She may be in danger."

Cassandra nearly told him then that Diana was present in the house and safe, but her tongue couldn't speak the words, for which she was grateful. At last she spoke. "Perhaps you will find her safe and sound before long."

Lord Basham took his leave, and Cassandra stood at the window to watch him climb in his carriage and go. She'd come very close to telling him all, which was totally unlike her. But truly, he seemed a perfect gentleman. Should she tell Quill about him? It didn't seem pertinent to anything, and she certainly didn't want to admit she'd nearly told his secret.

CHAPTER 14

Quill ordered Brutus saddled once he had packed his few belongings. Swinging up on the horse's back, his spirits lifted. He would see Anna Kate tomorrow.

When was her visit to Almack's to be? He had lost track of time, but he thought it was soon.

Lucas Cranford also weighed on his mind. The man was in a rage, a large part of it directed at himself. He blamed himself for all of Diana's troubles, rightly or wrongly.

When Rutledge abducted Diana nearly two years before, Lucas decided Diana must not want him, instead of giving her the benefit of a doubt. Perhaps he would have done the same thing in Lucas's place. In fact, had he failed to give Anna the benefit of a doubt too?

The thought spurred him on. He feared pushing the horse too much in the dark. There was a full moon, but clouds raced across it and, at times, obscured it completely. Once the storm arrived, there would be no light, and the road more dangerous. The temperature was dropping too.

He had passed a village some moments before. Because he could still see a few feet and because the storm hadn't fully arrived yet, he had decided not to stop. Now he regretted that decision.

Clouds completely obscured the moon, and rain began to fall, large, cold, wet drops. Before long, it turned to needles of ice, slashing at his face. *Not such a good idea to leave tonight*, he thought. He regretted bringing Brutus out, even though he knew the horse was tougher than he was himself. The rutted road turned rapidly to mud, but it wasn't cold enough for the mud to freeze quickly. He kept urging Brutus on, so they could reach someplace soon. The conditions were treacherous.

He thought there were probably three more miles ahead of him to the next village. He could not remember, but he hoped it had a decent inn.

He kept his head lowered, pulled down into the collar of his greatcoat. He tried to keep his eye on the verge of the road, so he would know if it turned from the present straight course. It was hard to see anything now, however, so he merely hoped and prayed the horse would carry him aright.

Icy rain dripped down his collar. He shivered. The wind was picking up, and he felt as though it was trying to help him out of his seat, as well as out of his coat. He sighed. This was going to be a trying journey.

Several yards down the road, Brutus lifted his head and whinnied. He heard something. He nodded his head up and down, telling Quill something was up.

Now he danced a bit, lifting his hooves and twitching his back end around, wanting to go off the road to the right. Quill scowled, squinting in hopes of being able to see through the falling rain. Nothing, but he did think he caught a whiff of a coal fire. Perhaps there was a house off the road, and Brutus knew it before he did. That was sensible. He could smell rotting straw, from stables, he was sure, for he also smelled manure. He gave Brutus his head, and they left the roadway.

Interesting how a dark night kept one from seeing but not from smelling.

Or hearing. He heard a grunt and the slam of a door, still off to his right. Brutus continued to act up, as though he recognized something or someone.

Quill bore on, until at last he saw a lighted window. He heaved a sigh. Shelter, at least, although not very elegant accommodations, of that he was sure.

He slid stiffly out of his saddle. He was nearly frozen, after such a short time on the road. How long since he'd left, only two hours or so? He didn't know and couldn't guess.

Quill led Brutus up near the house. It was fairly

large, perhaps ten rooms or so, more promising than he'd thought just moments before. There was a porte-cochere at the door, where he could leave Brutus out of the rain for a while, until he learned whether he would be offered the hospitality of the house.

He shook much of the rain off his coat and his hat, then raised the knocker. No one came for several minutes, so he tried again, punching the knocker as hard as he could against the brass base. At last the knob turned, and before him stood a tall young man with greasy hair stiff, like yellow straw. The face under the hair was healing from a severe beating, but he could see the fine lines of the man's bone structure. The clothes on his back were dandified, but the man in them was no dandy, not now.

"I'd forgotten already how badly Rutledge beat you," Quill said softly.

It was Lucas Cranford, with a tortured face and glaring eyes. "So, did you follow me here?" he said with a snarl.

"Cranford, you know better." Quill began to stick his hand out to touch the man gently on his arm, so sad did he feel for this hulk, but he refrained. "No, I just happened on to the house." He paused. "Actually, I think Brutus recognized your horse. He led me here. May I come in out of the rain? And may I stable my horse? It's raining worse than the plague out here."

"You're sure you are not here to spy on me?"

"Great racing Jehus, man, I had no idea you were here, or even that there was a house here. How could I be spying on you?" He paused, gestured inward in hopes Lucas would wake up and let him in. "It is cold out here, Cranford."

Lucas shook himself, as though just coming to his senses. "Oh, sorry, of course. I'll send my man around for the horse. He can put him up for you."

"Thank you." Quill followed him down the dark hall to a well-lit kitchen that smelled of roast beef and ale. "It smells delicious," he said, figuring Lucas would need a large hint to realize his guest was famished.

Lucas turned to him with a tight smile. "You are hungry."

"You might say that." Quill removed his coat and hat and laid them across the hearth near the fire. The smell of wet wool assailed his nose. Then he took a large white pottery mug off the large wooden table in the middle of the room, checked the inside of it to see if it was clean, then helped himself to coffee.

"Sugar or cream?" Lucas asked, now seeming to remember his manners. "Over there on the window ledge"

"Thanks."

Lucas leaned against the mantel and watched Quill put sugar and cream in the mug. He seemed to be weighing his next action. "So. You are not spying on me. I have to admit, in my right mind, you have never been a sneak, long as I have known you."

Quill bowed his head slightly and said, "Thank you."

"So how did you find me?"

Quill scowled at him. "I told you already. I was trying to return to London. I failed to stop at the last village, thinking I could keep on. Then the rain moved in, and I could see nothing. I wondered how I could continue, how my horse could keep his footing in the muck, when he led me to a dwelling here. And that is how I found you." He grinned, trying to disarm Lucas's suspicion. "Of course, I didn't know you were missing. How long have you been here?" He lifted the steaming mug to his lips and sipped, carefully.

Lucas still examined him. "All right. I believe you. You have been with Diana with the Austens for the past few days. How is she?"

"She is improving rapidly."

"A piece of good news, at least."

Quill grunted in agreement, then sat down at the table, even though he hadn't been invited to.

"This is a hunting lodge that belongs to a distant cousin. I decided to take advantage of its proximity to Godmersham." Lucas pulled away from the mantel and got himself a mug of coffee, which he placed on the table. Then he served Quill a large plate of beef, pickled beets, fresh bread, butter, and cheese.

"I see you have procured yourself a good cook."

Lucas held his mug up as if in a toast. "Only the best for Cranford, baron of Breckin." His tone was cynical.

Quill decided not to speak. Silence would likely pull information out of Lucas, better than more questions. He was too hungry to put off tackling the plate of food before him anyway.

About ten minutes passed. The clock in the hall chimed eleven. It was later than Quill had realized. No wonder he was so tired.

He finished the food, helped himself to another mug of coffee, with less sugar and cream this time, then yawned widely. The drowsy warmth and a full stomach began to lull him to sleep. Still Lucas did not speak, but merely sat staring into his mug.

At last Quill, pushing his chair back with a loud squawk on the stone floor, stood. "I do thank you for your hospitality. Do you have an extra room where I can sleep a few hours? I want to reach London within the next day or two, God willing. I have hopes for a clear day tomorrow."

Lucas snorted. "You have hopes, huh? I have none. But yes, there is an extra room for you."

"Will you go to London with me, Cranford? I am concerned about your state of mind."

"You're concerned! I am frightened out of my poor skull, frightened by the thoughts of revenge and death that occupy it."

This time Quill did reach out to put his hand

on the man's shoulder. "Lucas, please. Let me help you. You are torturing yourself."

Lucas turned sunken eyes to the childhood friend he'd always admired. This close, Quill could smell the reek of alcohol on his breath. "Don't you opine I deserve to be tortured?"

"Hardly, man. Snap out of it." He shook Lucas's shoulder roughly.

At last the other man's eyes cleared. "All right. I will come with you to London." He heaved a sigh, then paused. "Why am I coming with you?"

Quill shook his head. "To get well, to get your old spirit back so you can fight again. Diana will need your help soon. I know she is still very fond of you. I do not know what the judge will say about Rutledge's lies, or how she will get free of him, but some day she will perhaps be able to marry again. I would say she hopes you will be next to her when that day arrives."

Lucas shook his head, despair on his face. "That doesn't seem possible, ever."

"It is, but it won't be easy. Buck up—she'll need you strong and bold again."

The next day dawned clear but cold. Ice covered the water standing in ruts out in front of Cranford's house. With no cloud cover to hold in the earth's heat, the temperatures had plummeted. Quill could not decide, once he'd risen, dressed, and eaten, whether it was wise to start back on the road.

Lucas's condition concerned him. The man had surely been living on brandy for the past few days. He looked pale and weak and stumbled when he tried to rise from his chair that morning.

Should he take an extra day to nourish the man, so he wouldn't catch his death out in the cold air?

When Lucas began vomiting blood soon after breakfast, Quill knew he had his answer. But one day would not be enough. Lucas might take days to get back on his feet.

Quill wanted to take up the large crystal brandy decanter, now nearly empty, and throw it at the fireplace, so angry was he at the frustration of his plans. Yet he could not leave Lucas as he was.

He ordered Lucas's manservant to bring him fresh eggs and cream. He made an eggnog to speed Lucas on to recovery. No matter how much time it took for Lucas to get well, it would be too long. He longed to return to London and to see Anna Kate again.

Late in the day, after he'd given up hope for Lucas to make a speedy recovery for a departure the next day, he let his mind roam to Anna in London. He was sure that her appearance at Almack's was to be the next day. In the image that came to his mind she was wearing that rose velvet dress she'd worn that first day he'd seen her after so long a time. He didn't know a lot about women's fashions, but he knew that rose shade set off her skin, making it look like fresh, dewy roses itself. Her fresh scent reminded him of roses also. And her hair...

With a sigh he dragged himself back to the present time and place. He had duties: Lucas to see to, and then the big issue, changing the hideous law that could send someone like Diana off into exile. He was not going to be reduced to a mooncalf, even over Anna Kate Forsythe!

CHAPTER 15

On Thursday, after a late breakfast, Anna Kate joined Constance in the morning room. She still hoped her guilty conscience, from having gone out on her own to spy on Rutledge, wouldn't show on her face.

Constance didn't seem to notice. "Good morning, Anna. I have a letter from Cassandra Austen. Apparently that is where Quill took Diana. Quill left there three days ago, she says, and she is concerned because of the ice storm that hit that night. Their roads are barely passable. Yet they must be clear now—her letter got through."

"He's not with them? Where is he?"

"She writes that he said he was coming back to London. That's all."

"Back to London? Could he have returned and not have come to call? That is possible, and likely. He doesn't owe me an accounting for his actions. I am quite sure he doesn't guess I am outrageously curious."

"Outrageous indeed. I should say that if he is back in London, you will hear from him." Constance paused. "There is, by the way, one more short sentence."

Anna pulled her attention back to Constance from her worry over Quill's safety as well as her anxiety that he'd returned without calling on her. "Yes?"

Constance smiled warmly at her friend. "She adds she and Jane found him to be a man charmingly in love with some beautiful young miss in London, an 'Anna,' they say."

Anna squealed, then dashed across to snatch at the letter. "Oh, you were teasing me with that bit of news, were you not? Let me see it!"

"Now, now, let us see only ladylike behavior here," Constance said, holding the letter back, still taunting, but kindly so.

"Oh, Constance, I cannot bear this uncertainty. He drives me wild, not letting me know for sure what his feelings are. This is a horrible state to be in, and I hope never to find myself in it again!"

Constance looked at the letter in her hands. "It will end happily for you, I feel sure. My understanding is that he is honorable. He seems to care for you, and you certainly care for him. Try to hold on to your sanity for a few more weeks."

"Weeks!"

"Or even days. I believe you will have a pleasing proposal before long."

Anna covered her cheeks with her hands, her eyes wide with uncertainty and longing. "You know something?"

"No, not at all, except for the ways of a man with a young miss." She rose. "I must see to the children's lessons. Even though Mother Stanfield is fond of overseeing them herself, I still believe I must keep my hand in." She handed Anna Kate the letter, then patted her on the arm.

Moving her chair nearer to the window in the morning room, Anna sat down to read the letter over and over. Then she looked out at the melting snow and ice. She could picture in her mind just how bad the roads in the country would be. Truthfully, however, she knew Quill could make his way through them; *she* could if she were motivated enough.

That thought set the wheels in motion: perhaps she should order up the carriage and go call on Lady Wentworth. She hadn't seen her since the late meal after the day in court. Hopping up from her seat, she made her way out of the morning room and up to the children's schoolroom to find Constance.

Mary greeted her beloved Anna Kate. "Come see the new picture book Grandmama has brought us. Will you read it to us?" It was a beautifully illustrated version of *Jack the Giant Killer*.

Anna leaned over to hug the exuberant child. "I will dearly love to read it to you. It looks charming." She kept one arm around Mary and greeted Paul. "How is the pony training coming?"

He grimaced. "That old mare may never learn a single trick Lord Wentworth's horse knows. It is quite disgusting."

She laughed. "It takes time, you know, for anything of value to come about."

Constance looked at her and winked, surreptitiously so the children couldn't see. "Yes, that is the very truth."

Anna nodded discreetly to Constance, a small smile on her face, to show she took Constance's point. Then she sat down to read the book to Mary, while knowing Paul was listening in the background. She guessed he did not want anyone to know a young man such as he would find a child's picture book interesting. He even laughed when the giant fell to his rather dramatic death.

Once she was through reading, she took a few moments to hug both children and ask for their news. The biggest piece of news was that they planned to skate on a nearby pond, now that it had turned cold.

Anna glanced out the window where icicles dripped steadily. "Today? I vow you will not skate today." Mary's small, expressive face fell, so Anna hastened to say, "But winter isn't over. I am sure you will skate on the pond before March arrives."

With those words she kissed them good bye. "I would like to go visit Lady Wentworth, if that is all right with you, Constance."

"Oh, but you must rest! You go to Almack's tonight."

"I won't stay long. I can't rest until I know whether Quill has arrived safely back in town."

"As long as two footmen accompany you. But don't stay long."

Her words brought back to Anna Kate her guilty secret. She knew she'd been fortunate not to get caught by Rutledge; the next time she sneaked out, she'd disguise herself as a man.

The short drive to Wentworth House left Anna nearly breathless. She was anxious to see Quill, but also afraid of his reaction to her forwardness. She decided to act as though she had given his whereabouts no thought, that this visit was purely social.

Eleanor greeted her with great warmth. "My dear, I am so glad to see you. The past days have gone so slowly, with no young people in the house." She gestured to Anna to give Randall her cloak.

Anna's heart dropped and her resolve to dissemble about her motives fled. "So Quill is not back?"

"No, sadly enough. I have no word of him since before the storm."

Anna Kate quickly told her of the letter Constance had received that morning. "Do you think he had an accident or fell ill?" she asked, her hands twisting her handkerchief between them.

Lady Wentworth glanced out the window, toward the east in the direction of Kent and Godmersham. "That is possible, but no, I don't believe it. Quill is much too cautious about himself and careful of his horseflesh to run the risk of an accident."

She beckoned to Anna to come sit by the fire. Anna sat for a moment, deep in thought, then she said to Lady Wentworth, "I feel I should go to him. He may need help."

"Nonsense!" she said forcefully. "How would you ever find him? He has left Diana with the Austens; you have no idea where he may be now."

"But Miss Austen said he was coming back to London. He hasn't arrived. What could be wrong?"

"Perhaps nothing is wrong." She sat a bit taller. "Anna Kate, I must strongly discourage you from considering this course. If nothing else, you must consider Quill's dignity. He would not appreciate a young miss coming to search him out, to save him from some unknown fate. Why, he'd be a laughingstock."

Anna slumped in her seat. "You're right, of course. My heart misled my head again. And," she added, a rueful look on her face, "only think how angry he'd be with me if I made him look foolish." She got up and began to walk around the room. "Oh, I cannot think for thinking about him. You must find me very foolish."

Eleanor smiled. "Yes, quite so, but I do remember being young myself."

"Young! That is what everyone says of me. Why can no one ever mention how very mature I am?"

"They will when you are older. Now, please stop prowling around like a tiger in his cage. Sit down and have a bit of tea. You surely have some news for me about your upcoming visit to Almack's." Eleanor poured them both cups of tea.

Anna grimaced. "Yes, it is tonight."

"Tonight!"

"Quite. I have several lovely new dresses, and I can take no pleasure in any of them. Some young subaltern is accompanying me tonight, a friend of Toby Esterby's. He is very flattering, the way he stares at me so." She dropped two sugars in her cup. "I will either correct him for behaving like a schoolboy, or fall for him. He is charming and even handsome."

They continued to talk in a desultory fashion for the next thirty minutes. At last Anna put down her cup and said, "I have enjoyed being able to come here and talk with you, my lady. Thank you for your great kindness to me."

"It is my pleasure, my dear. You are charming company." Eleanor rose. "Do come again. We can each help the other while away the time until he returns. And next time you will be able to tell me small tidbits about Almack's."

"You're the one who got me this voucher, aren't

you?"

"No, actually it was Quill himself. He seems to know Lady Jersey somewhat."

Anna blushed. She hoped that bit of news did not mean what it often did when a man was reputed to know the woman well.

Eleanor put a hand on Anna's arm. "Don't worry. He doesn't womanize. He is much too sober for that."

"Forgive me for my bluntness, but would a mother know?"

"Believe me, my dear, a mother would know."

Once again Anna thanked the dignified older woman for her graciousness, then took her leave. Her mind was somewhat at ease about Quill's safety, for Lady Wentworth was so serene about him. She returned glad she had been so bold as to visit the countess.

Anna was not able to rest that afternoon. She thought she would scream before the day was over. She did discipline herself to write to her father as well as to the three students who had written her from home. She was thankful at least for the duty, so she could relegate her worries to the back of her mind.

Mary and Paul came to her room late in the afternoon. "Anna Kate," Mary asked shyly, "will you come see the pony? Perhaps you can teach her her lessons."

Glad for the distraction, she dressed the children in their outdoor clothes, then put on her own cloak and pattens. They each picked up carrots on their way out through the kitchen.

The pony greeted them with a whinny. Paul brought her out of her stall and put her harness on. "We want her to just bob her head up and down. You'd think it would be an easy thing for her to learn."

Anna took the carrot from inside her sleeve and held it out to the small mare, but not close enough she could actually take it. "Hold her so she cannot step forward, but loose enough that she can move her head." Moving the carrot up above the pony's head, Anna succeeded in making her reach up for it. Then she quickly pulled it down below the pony's neck, and the pony bowed to try to snatch it from her hand. Soon she had the children in gales of laughter as they watched the pony bob her head up and down, trying to get the carrot from Anna's hand. At last she let the mare have the carrot. "You'll quit trying if you never succeed, won't you?"

They soon tired of playing with the pony, for which Anna was grateful. She wanted to walk in the neighborhood before complete dark fell.

Taking Mary by the hand and with Paul on her heels, Anna walked up the lane to the main street. She wanted to run and shout, the way she had as a child. Yet, if she were still a child, Quill would definitely have no romantic interest in her. It was better to be a young woman now, even in spite of the frustrations and setbacks.

Once back inside, she did think of a solution to her concern for Quill. She sent for Toby, who arrived just before dinner.

"No, Anna, I haven't seen him, and I don't believe he'd come to town without speaking to me. Nor to you, for that matter. You're sure Miss Austen knew what she was saying?"

"Wasn't he staying with them at Godmersham?"

"Yes, of course."

"Then how could he be missing within their house?" She began to pace around the drawing room. "Something is wrong, very wrong. You have to find him, or I'll have to."

Toby's mouth fell open. "How can you find him? You're a young lady. If he's missing, it won't be in a drawing room in Mayfair!"

"Excuse me," she said, drawing herself up. "I really am not so frivolous I know only of drawing rooms, you know."

"Sorry, sorry. I didn't mean to insult you." He pulled at his lower lip as he thought. "Look, let me set some sort of search in train. We both have this outing to Almack's tonight to get through, and I'll do my best to find him myself afterwards, if he doesn't turn up before. I promise."

She stared at him as she considered his plan. "All right. For now. Then I'll look for him myself."

After dinner Anna returned to her room for a hot bath and the long process of having her hair dressed. Susan Travis was no longer the children's seamstress, now having moved up to being Anna's maid. Tonight, as usual, Susan kept to silence, unless Anna asked her a specific question.

Once Anna was out of the tub and wrapped in several large, warmed towels, she spoke. "You're so restful for a fuss-budget like me, Susan. I do wish I had your gift of silence."

"Thank you, miss. Others have berated me for being too dull."

"Who would that be?"

"My aunt for one—my mother's sister. She told me I would never land a husband if I did not try to chatter as the Quality do. I can't learn it, however."

"Oh, my, the same old plaint. We must be good man bait, must we not? So much of our time and efforts directed toward being just so to please the men."

"Yes, miss."

"Foolishly I thought only a fright like me would have to be trained and pushed and pulled to be made over into someone worthy of a man's notice. Somehow, I thought someone like you would find a man so easily and naturally."

"Not quite, Miss Anna. There is someone, but because he is a servant in another household, we must not see each other for fear of our master or mistress learning of it and then fearing the loss of our services." She paused. "I tell you this in confidence, miss. My job would be lost me if anyone knew."

Anna kept her tongue at first. She knew she might say something much too radical. British aristocrats still feared too much familiarity, for fear it would breed revolution as it had in France. "I pray that you and your 'someone' can work it out so you may marry."

Susan blushed. "Thank you, miss," she said quietly, then went about her business of helping Anna dress in her undergarments and then doing her hair.

The warm golden brown hair, with its silky luster, fell smoothly into curls as Susan did up Anna's hair. She wound the thick locks up over Anna's right ear, and then arranged the curls into a cascade over the right shoulder.

At last she slipped the rose silk dress over Anna's shoulders. "It's beautiful, miss," she said.

Anna examined her reflection carefully. She was pleased with how the color set off her skin, hair, and eyes. She sighed. "I do wish Quill were the one taking me tonight."

"Yes, miss, I understand."

Death in Exile

Looking in the mirror once more, she nodded in approval. "The dress is much more modest than most will be at Almack's, I am sure," she said with a smile, "but that suits a vicar's daughter like me."

CHAPTER 16

Sir Matthew Dunstable arrived at ten to take Anna Kate to Almack's. Constance had lent her a full-length ermine cape to wear. "I feel a princess tonight," Anna said with a shy smile.

"And you look the loveliest one in the universe," Constance said, with Sir Matthew's approval. "Your eyes will rival Almack's hostesses' diamonds." She kissed Anna on the cheek. "Have a wonderful evening."

Sir Toby and his young lady, Camilla Drayton-Day, were in the carriage when Matthew handed Anna in the door. Toby, his red hair fighting against its latest combing to return to its natural spikiness, greeted Anna but with no word of his search for Quill. Anna spoke to Camilla, who said not a word.

Anna's first reaction to Camilla was curiosity at her silence, but during the drive to the assembly, she decided Camilla was merely very young and frightened with it. She tried to warm the girl up for the evening, so Camilla's first outing to such a prestigious place would be enjoyable in spite of her own worry about Quill.

Toby seemed quite smitten with Camilla, a slim girl with black hair and striking green eyes. Anna was glad for him. Camilla wore an emerald green gown that played up her eyes. Anna complimented her on the dress, but the girl did not respond.

In spite of it being early in the Season, there was quite a crush in Almack's when they arrived. The swirl of colors and of dazzling stones, of dashing men in well-cut jackets and spotless trousers and ladies with plump, creamy arms and shoulders quite amazed Anna. Had she ever seen so much flesh? She turned to Camilla, who hung on Toby's arm with a closed look on her face. "I do not believe I have ever seen such an assemblage of well-fed and well-dressed people in all my life."

The girl turned a look of disgust on her. "Really?" she said, her tone hateful. "You do not get about much."

Shocked at how badly she had misjudged Camilla, Anna forced herself to smile. Matthew moved in close, as if to protect Anna, who said, "No, I do not. I am only a poor vicar's daughter, you understand."

The sneer on Camilla's face was maddening. Anna wanted to slap her, but decided that would not become a vicar's daughter.

Camilla spoke, raising her voice as though she

wanted those around her to hear: "You know, Miss Forsythe, I do not believe I have ever heard of your being presented at Court."

"You are right. I have not been."

Camilla smiled a cobra smile. "Then how is it you come to be here? You must be presented first before you are ever considered for a voucher to Almack's."

Anna flinched. The widgeon was correct. She knew that, as she was sure Aunt Lydia and Lady Wentworth also knew. What had happened that she was allowed here? A mistake? Would Camilla get her thrown out as an impostor?

Matthew squeezed her elbow and led her away before she could come up with some reply. "You have not heard of Camilla Drayton-Day, I take it."

"Not until Toby mentioned her that day at the Stanfields'." She glanced at his face to see how he had taken Camilla's snub of her.

He seemed unfazed. "She is quite the most thorough-going snob in town. I know—I was affianced to her for a short time."

Turning wide eyes up to examine his face for hidden feelings, she saw only a mild amusement there. She looked over her shoulder at Camilla, who was hanging on to Toby as though he were a lifebuoy. "She is very lovely."

"Hmph," he said. He took her right hand and placed his hand on the small of her back. "Come, let me introduce you to the ladies who run this place." Leading her around the throngs filling the room, he went on. "How well do you know Toby?"

"Only a bit." She began to feel faint from the crush, the heat, and the heady perfumes in the room. "Why?"

"The little I know of him tells me he is too fine a chap to be used by such as dear Camilla."

Anna scowled, then stopped their forward progress to the edge of the room where Lady Jersey and her coterie sat chatting and laughing. "But—?"

"What?"

"Toby is a fine catch, I am sure, but he is only a knight. He has no hereditary title and only a soldier's pay. Why does she pursue him?"

He turned to smile at her. He really did have the most charming smile she had seen in a long time. "Didn't you know? She is not pursuing Toby, but a friend of his. She plans to use him to get to the friend."

A chill hand of fear gripped Anna's throat. "A friend of Toby's?" she forced out.

"Yes, Lord Wentworth, of course."

Blood rushed from her head. She swayed a bit from the heat and press, and from Matthew's news. "Of course," she whispered.

He scrutinized her face. "Anna? Are you all right? You look pale as death."

She pressed one hand against her forehead. "I apologize. So silly of me, but I feel faint. From the heat and the perfume..."

Death in Exile

Solicitous now, he frowned, then put one arm around her shoulders. "Let me take you out for some air. It's quite close in here."

"Close, yes," she repeated, weakly. She allowed him to support her as he made his way to one of the open doors where she could catch a breath of air.

The air was brittle and cold, and she gasped once he'd led her outside. "I ought to go get your fur. You will catch your death out here."

She gripped his hand. "Oh, don't leave me." She was trembling, and she struggled to control it.

He smiled cozily at her and moved in closer. Wrapping his arms about her, he whispered in her hair, "I will attempt to serve as your greatcoat for a few moments if you wish."

She jerked away. "No! I mean, thank you for your thoughtfulness, but I do not wish to be among the latest *on-dits* tomorrow. My father would be mortified if I were to get a name for being fast." She turned away. "Please, Matthew, I am sorry, but take me back inside. I feel very foolish, but what Camilla said is true. I do not get about much, and I am not used to the crush of people. I will take a deep breath and steel myself to the crowd and the heat and the noise, so you do not have to worry yourself about me. I really am quite a strong, healthy person."

"Good," he said huskily as he briefly embraced her one more time. "Your hair smells lovely."

She nearly ran back into the assembly rooms.

Charming Sir Matthew was more than she had bargained for. Did Quill suspect he would behave this way?

She corrected herself. Quill had asked Toby to squire her here; it was Toby who had palmed her off on Matthew. *Oh, dear,* she thought, *I am not sufficiently accustomed to the ways of Society. Why did I think I could merely come and look around, and then go home and forget it all? This whole undertaking reeks with undercurrents of meaning, of power, and—yes, I must say the word—even sexuality, things I am not conversant in. Oh, dear,* she repeated to herself.

Matthew seemed oblivious to her chagrin. "Would you care for some orgeat? It's dreadful stuff, but all we will get here, I wager."

"No, thank you, tea, if possible." Perhaps he would leave her for few moments so she could catch her breath and her aplomb.

Matthew left her standing near a wall. She wished she were a small mouse in the corner, observing the company.

To her untutored eyes the people there looked rather odd. The men were handsome and the women beautiful, but it all struck her as too much of everything. Her frugal upbringing contrasted so strongly with the wealth and show around her. She sighed. She ought to be quite over the moon at being included in such an assemblage, but in reality she felt sated, even sickened, as though she had eaten too much rich food. She was hopeless, a snob in reverse, because she disliked the ostentation.

Within moments Matthew returned with two cups of tea. She took a cup from him and sniffed. She made a face. "Rather rancid, is it not?"

He threw his head back and laughed, which made several people standing near look askance at them. "Priceless."

She blushed, then raised her cup to take a sip. Over the edge of the cup she saw a tall man with black hair enter the assembly room. His eyes—she couldn't see them from this distance, but she knew they were a stunning green—raked the assembled throngs, as though he were looking for someone of import to him.

Her heart played funny, first lifting in joy, then falling in despair. "He is here," she said. "Camilla will be pleased."

"Who? Oh, Lord Wentworth. There she makes for him like a frigate for an enemy battleship. She will engage him in battle, and she will win."

Anna did not answer. She merely handed him her cup.

CHAPTER 17

Anna Kate's first reaction to Matthew's assurance that Camilla would win Quill was a sick acceptance. Yes, she believed the hateful miss would attain her goal.

Then, however, her second reaction took even her by surprise. With a deep breath, she stood ramrod straight. In her mind's eye she saw a bull in a nearby farmer's field when she was a child. When that bull was provoked, it would snort, paw one foot, then charge. Right now she envisioned herself quite like that bull. She wanted to giggle. Her long skirts would probably get in the way of her charging feet.

To Matthew she smiled, then patted him on the arm. "You know, I'm not so sure about that. I would recommend to you—if you hear of book being made on it—be quite sure to bet against Camilla."

"Miss Forsythe?" he asked, his tone confused.

"What...?"

She didn't hear the rest of his sentence. He was a very nice young man, and she imagined she was being discourteous, but she would not roll over and play dead. If she had any chance, the remotest chance, of winning Quill, she was going to fight for it. Besides, she'd been too worried about him during his delay in returning to town.

In Anna's traverse of the crowded room, she kept her eyes on Quill, on his face. He was like the North Star, her star to guide her path. Once he saw Camilla, her path would be set forever, for Anna dreaded what she might see on his face. His expression when he looked at the young, beautiful, snobbish Camilla would tell her precisely how much chance she had with him.

She saw Toby trailing in Camilla's wake. He looked completely befuddled. She heard Camilla call Quill's name. She saw Quill stop and swivel his head around to the direction whence the call had come.

Then she saw his face. His visage turned as black with fury as ever she had seen, even when he had been so angry with her over Diana that first day. The scowl was fierce enough to blast away the coldest north wind. The scowl froze, then faded. On his face was displayed the blandest expression ever to be assumed by any of the Quality.

Then she watched as his eyes slid over and past Camilla, to Toby behind her. He did not speak to her, but he bellowed to his friend, "Toby, my man, so good to see you in this sad crush. You look quite the Corinthian tonight."

Anna wanted to fly off into gales of laughter. Never had she seen a cut direct done so well. Nor, she vowed, had Camilla, who now stood, mouth hanging open, staring after Quill's retreating back.

He grabbed Toby by one arm and rushed him through the press to the wall near where Anna had been standing not moments before. Toby seemed to be spluttering and gesticulating, and Quill looked like a slab of granite poised to start an avalanche.

She hurried to return to her previous spot, where Matthew was chatting with a bevy of five young women who were giggling and hanging on his every word. In her brief pass by him, she thought she could learn a thing or two about flirting from those young women. What a shame she didn't have the time.

She slowed her headlong rush once she reached a spot about five feet from Quill. He was hissing in Toby's ear. "Surely you recall a simple request, my explicitly asking you, not some soldier and stranger, to escort Miss Forsythe here, Sir Toby?"

"Well, yes, Quill, but..."

"So why is she in the company of someone else, and why are you in the company of that—" Here he broke off. Anna was thankful. She did not wish to hear what he might call the woman.

"I...I'm dreadful sorry, Quill, but she begged me. How could I refuse such a lovely lady's entreaty?"

"Where is Anna?"

"I am right here, Quill," she said pertly.

He turned such a malevolent glare on her that she nearly quailed. Instead she smiled. "It is lovely to see you, Quill. I had worried so when we heard you had left Kent in the storm."

He did not smile, but he let go of Toby and put one arm protectively around her. The orchestra had begun a waltz. "Will you honor me with this dance, Miss Forsythe? I have secured permission for you to waltz."

She blushed. Somehow that didn't seem possible, since she wasn't even supposed to be here, not having been presented at Court yet. But she would not quibble. "Certainly, milord." She turned her head aside, her neck arching like a swan's. For the moment, at least, she felt dignified enough for anyone to look at her and judge her.

He pulled her as close as good manners would allow and whispered in her hair, "You are beautiful, Anna Kate."

She turned her head just a trifle so his mouth was at her cheek. "Thank you, milord."

He tightened his grip on her precipitately, enough so that she gasped. He growled low in her ear, "Do not call me 'milord.' You know it drives me mad."

"Yes, sir, I apologize. But when you look so fierce, I am frightened and cannot think of anything else to call you."

Pulling away from her so he could gaze into her face, he asked, "Do you really expect me to believe that of you?" As he looked at her, his face softened. "I do not believe you're afraid of anything, and in particular, not of me." His voice deepened, and he pulled her closer.

She couldn't breathe. She wished she could melt into his arms and never leave their strength, warmth, and protection. She nestled her head under his chin. "Oh, Quill," she sighed.

"What, my sweet?"

"I wish..."

"You wish what?"

She sighed again. "I wish we could always stay this way. It feels so safe here in the circle of your arms."

Quill gathered her a little closer. "This is lovely, but I do not want to endanger your good name," he whispered. "Perhaps we should appear more distant."

She snuggled in closer, then sighed a third time. "Yes, I am sure you are right." But she didn't pull back.

He laughed softly, his breath stirring the tendrils of hair around her face. "You little minx."

This time she did pull away a bit, in order to see his face. "Do you hate the fact we used to be friends when we were children? Does that make me seem—oh, too familiar?"

His face gave nothing away. In graceful turns he led her away from the dancing couples in the middle of the floor and to doors opening outside. "You look warm," he said, in way of explanation.

Once they were outside, she asked, "Well?"

"Well what?" His old scolding tone was back.

"Do I seem too familiar so that you scorn me?"

He turned away to lean against the balustrade. Looking out over the twinkling lights of the city, he hesitated before answering. She could hardly breathe as she waited. "It is not that you are too familiar, it is that you are too bothersome."

She gasped. Somehow that epithet seemed worse to her than "familiar" did.

"I have a task before me, to try to reform the law concerning transportation, and you interrupt my concentration." He straightened, turning back to gaze into her eyes. "You are much, much too enticing, Miss Forsythe." He pulled her gently to him and kissed her tenderly, then again, more deeply. "You are lovely," he said gruffly, sending her blood racing.

"Quill." She reached her arms up around his neck and returned his kisses, not too demurely. "Am I too forward?" she asked, then kissed him again.

"Delightfully so." He kissed her one more time, then cleared his throat. "Anna Kate, this is not a good idea. My mother and your aunt have laid all these fabulous plans for your Season, and it will end before it begins if we go on this way." He still held her in his arms, and he moved on to kissing her hair, then her throat.

"Oh, Quill," she moaned, "I don't want a Season, I just want you." She pulled away. "Please don't despise me, but I cannot play the coquette. It is you I love, and only you."

He dropped his hands from her shoulders. "This poses a problem, Anna."

She chilled. "What?" She hoped she was hiding the panic in her voice, but she doubted it.

"I cannot express it, not simply. I feel I must speak in the Lords about this horrendous situation. Diana has come so close to being found guilty and sent away. Think of the injustice that would be. In fact, we still are not clear of that threat."

Anna felt a twinge of jealousy, then renounced it. Quill loved Diana, as did she, in a different way from the way they loved one another. Diana was not a rival for his affections, but her plight was at the moment a rival for his time. "I understand," she said softly, so softly he had to bend closer to hear.

"What?"

"I understand." She rather liked having him so close, so she did not raise her voice much.

He kissed her again, gently, on the tip of her nose. "Such a pert nose, even if it is frequently pointed too high," he teased.

She giggled. "And you know another of my many failings, a dreadful tendency to giggle. My father has tried so hard to train it out of me."

"You have only one failing, my sweet," he said, kissing her on the lips once more. "You are too unsettling for a man who has a major task to perform, and for one with a regrettable tendency to showing his emotions, in this stiff-upper-lip culture of ours."

"Are you quite sure—only one failing, I mean? I thought I had myriads."

"No, just one." He enfolded her again in his arms and kissed her once more.

Just as Anna felt herself drowning in the depths of his kiss, they were suddenly interrupted by the arrival of a puffing Toby. "Quill," he said, "that is, Lord Wentworth! You must come back in. Camilla is raising a stink with Lady Jersey about Anna being here. You must come."

Quill snarled, or at least to Anna it sounded like a snarl. Toby quailed before the frown on Quill's face. "I'll be right there." He waved Toby back into the assembly room, then turned back for one last kiss. "Don't fret, little one. This will sort itself out, you'll see."

Letting her precede him, Quill escorted her back to Sir Matthew. He stared at him now; something nudged the edge of his brain about Matthew—what was it? He couldn't remember.

To Toby he said, "Take her home, you and Dunstable both. I will be along later."

"What about Camilla?" Toby spluttered, a horrified look on his face.

"I will sort out Camilla, never you fear. I'll take her home, and she'll wish she had never heard the name Quill Rossiter in her life."

The thundercloud on his brow convinced Anna he would do as he said, but what would that mean? She didn't want to think about it.

Matthew had rescued Constance's ermine cloak, and he now draped it around Anna's shoulders. He smiled that charming smile again.

"You are not angry with me, going off with someone else?" Anna asked with a blush. "I am sorry. I am not typically..." She stopped there. She didn't want to say the word for what others might label her behavior of the evening. "It is merely that Lord Wentworth is an old childhood chum."

"Did he always mess your hair so much when you were childhood chums?" Matthew asked, no ill humor in his tone.

"Oh!" Now Anna really blushed. Touching her hair, in an attempt to straighten it, she wondered if her face would become permanently red from all the emotions that had left their mark on her too-expressive visage.

The drive back to the Stanfields' house was torment for Anna Kate. First of all, Toby was embarrassed, and Matthew was amused. She thought she would grow tired of his perennial good humor if she had to spend much time in his company.

She had no idea of what Quill would say or how Lady Jersey would take it. She could only imagine his offending Almack's patroness. He did have a tendency to be outspoken. She imagined that by noon today—for it was now 2 AM on the Thursday—her name would be a byword.

Oh, my. What will Papa say? And Lady Wentworth—she will never accept as a daughter-in-law a girl who was the cause of scandal. She tried to look out the side window but could see nothing.

Soon they pulled up at the house. Both Toby and Matthew accompanied her to the front door. "I'm sorry, Anna Kate," Toby said, shamefaced, "for this farrago. Quill'll have my hide for this."

"Your apology is accepted. It's been a lovely evening—or at least very interesting."

Matthew patted her on the back as though she were a pal. "That's the spirit. We can always look on the bright side."

"Easy for you to say, Dunstable," Toby snapped. "You won't have to defend your head against Wentworth!"

Chapter 18

Constance was waiting for Anna when she got home. She kissed the young woman on the cheek and said, "How was Almack's?"

Anna grimaced. "I don't know where to begin. It was quite different from what I expected." She handed the ermine cloak to the butler, who looked unhappy to be up in the middle of the night.

Eyes bright, Constance said, "Tell me all."

"I imagine Camilla is the best place to start." She regaled Constance with Camilla's behavior. "I don't believe I have ever seen Quill so angry, not even with me. And then, when he gave her the cut direct! I have heard of it before, but never actually seen it." She took Constance's hands and said earnestly, "Tell me, does it indicate poor character in me to gloat so over seeing the little snip brought low?"

Constance laughed. "Quite poor. But amusing."

Anna didn't tell her about the kisses on the

promenade outside the assembly room. Those she could not share.

"You know, this is dreadful, but I'm starving. Could I find myself something to eat?" Constance made to ring for the butler, but Anna stopped her. "Please let me get it myself. I know this is low-bred of me, but I would rather wait on myself."

Constance smiled, then said, "I'll keep you company. I'm somewhat peckish myself."

They worked together. "Cook will have a fit in the morning," Constance said as she heated milk.

Anna sliced bread and cheese and put out plates and mugs for them both.

They ate their bread and cheese and drank their mugs of warm milk in companionable silence. After washing up their dishes, they parted in the second-floor hall. Constance hugged Anna good night. "That reminded me of nights away at school when we girls would gossip in the night. The headmistress never seemed to find out," she said.

Anna Kate thought she would not be able to sleep once she had undressed with a sleepy Susan's aid and got in bed. She closed her eyes and tried to recall every precious moment with Quill, but once she got past the snubbing of Camilla and the being removed from the assemblage—once she got to the best part, the kisses—she fell asleep.

Quill approached Lady Jersey as nonchalantly as he could. His mind was spinning with the various things he could say to her.

He caught her eye when he was still some ten feet or so away and smiled somewhat sardonically. He decided perhaps the best attitude to take was one of amusement at the foolishness of some young women. Not all, of course. Lady Jersey was herself quite young.

Out of the corner of his eye he glimpsed Camilla Drayton-Day standing alone. He hoped her feelings were in tatters wondering what would happen to her. He hoped too that his ploy to leave her unaccompanied by her escort for the evening would unsettle her enough to make her pliable later.

What a miss she is, he thought. *I will be glad to see her comeuppance.* He gave her a glance intended to show indifference. When she narrowed her eyes and lifted her chin a fraction of an inch, he knew he had hit his target. He chuckled inwardly.

Then a movement behind Camilla Drayton-Day caught his eye. It was Lyndel Dunstable, Lord Basham, staring at him as if ready to accost him. What was he doing here? He wasn't an eligible young bachelor, for he'd been married to an old shrew for years.

So that was the odd note that had bothered him

earlier. His brother had accompanied Anna Kate. As far as he knew, Sir Matthew was harmless. But Basham? He was in league with Rutledge, a gambling and whoring partner with him. Quill would have to address that issue later.

Upon reaching Lady Jersey, seated at the head of the room with her coterie, he bowed over her hand and kissed it. "Lady Jersey, it is good to see you again."

Her smile was cool, but he had expected that. He knew her too well to think she would show what she was thinking.

This aristocratic disdain of warm emotions pervaded all of Society. Most of the time, it served Quill's purposes well, but it hadn't in the past few weeks. Anna and Diana, Rutledge's, Camilla's and Toby's behaviors—his feelings were continuously heated to the boiling point. He consciously tamped down the fires in his brain for this conversation with the patricians who ran Almack's.

"I am sure," Lady Jersey said.

Quill did not smile at the haughty tone in her voice, but it struck him as artifice, pure and simple. But he could play the game too, at least most of the time. "You have quite a delightful assemblage of people tonight, my lady."

She gazed languorously around the gathering of titles and jewels, silks and fine woolens. "Thank you." She shifted slightly on a small French bench, painted white with gilt trim. "I understand you are involved in a farrago involving a young miss who is not entitled to be at Almack's."

At that point Camilla joined them. Quill glanced at her face, which was smug and full of venom. "Oh, no, my lady. I believe Miss Camilla Drayton-Day has been invited quite properly."

He found great satisfaction in the hiss of displeasure that escaped Camilla's pouty young mouth. "I beg your pardon!" she said.

He straightened and looked her in the eye. Feigning innocence, he asked her, "Did I make a mistake? I did believe you had the right to be here."

"You know perfectly well I am not the person with a questionable claim to be here!" She had raised her voice, and her shrewish tones filled the room. All the party-goers fell silent, so her last words were heard by nearly all. Those who hadn't heard were asking others to repeat what had been said.

At that point Quill knew he had won the game, and he relaxed. His great fatigue from his efforts and travel of the past few days suddenly caught up with him, and he realized just how very tired he was.

A tall, portly lady sitting behind Lady Jersey slightly to her left stood and drew herself up to her full height, which was close to Quill's own, he was sure. She spoke with an echoing timbre to her voice. "To whom do we owe the pleasure of this disorder?"

If Quill were the type to shake in fear, surely

this damsel, near seventy years of age, would make him quiver now. Instead, he bowed slightly to her and said, a charming smile on his face, "Lady Dillman, how lovely to see you. I am sure my mother would have sent her regards had she known you would be here."

She raised her lorgnette to her eyes, which were sparkling now with pleasure, "Why, Lord Wentworth, how nice to see you." Lady Dillman, a distant relative of Quill's father, had always had a soft place in her heart for Quill, whom she had known—and spoiled with comfits—when he was a small boy. She now leaned forward and whispered in Lady Jersey's ear.

Lady Jersey nodded her head in understanding of whatever it was Lady Dillman had told her. Quill was sure it was to his credit. His parents' and his own honorable standards in the past always served him well, for which he was thankful. Little acts of chivalry, of kindness, added up.

His father had always been the epitome of integrity. Quill regretted his father's early death, for he had not told his father how much he, Quill, admired him. At the time, he had resolved not to let his mother end her time before he had told her how much she meant to him; so far he had not kept that resolution. He would rectify that tomorrow.

Camilla Drayton-Day interrupted his thoughts at that moment. "You have treated me most shamefully, Quillen Rossiter," she said, a whine in her voice. "You invite me here—"

"I never invited you. My friend did, not I."

She went on. "You turn me off in favor of your paramour, and now you shame me."

"My paramour? I beg your pardon," he said coldly. "I have no paramour, and even though this news will disappoint you, I will not be taking one either."

"Then just who was that common thing you were with earlier?"

"'Common thing'? Why, did you not recognize her? She was Miss Forsythe, the descendent of Guy Windesor. She is the soul of propriety, Miss Drayton-Day. Perhaps you do not recognize that either?" With those words, he turned back to Lady Jersey, Lady Dillman, and their friends. "I do regret this scene, my ladies. I will humbly beg your leave. I have had a long ride today and am suddenly overcome with fatigue. If you will excuse me." Again he sketched a bow and backed away from that powerful inner circle. He believed he had given them plenty of fodder for tomorrow's *on-dits*, and Anna Kate would not be among them.

He saw he was leaving them with a positive impression of himself. Lady Dillman even waggled her fingers at him in farewell.

To Camilla Drayton-Day he said not a word.

The frigid air outside cleared his head. *Camilla!* he thought. *I promised to be sure she got home.* He decided the most fitting thing would be to send

Toby for her, so he swung up on Brutus, once the
stabler handed the horse's reins to him, and made
his way to the Two Swans.

There he knocked at the inn door loud enough
to wake the dead. A sleepy porter came to the door.
"Why, you're not asleep on the job, are you?" Quill
teased.

"No, milord," the porter said miserably. His
eyes were streaming and his chest sounded con-
gested.

Quill took pity on him. "You sound as though
you've caught your death of cold. I'm sorry to disturb you. I'll go find Sir Toby myself."

Gritting his teeth, still angry with Toby and
Camilla for the evening's fiasco, he made his way
up the stairs to Toby's room. Fortunately, Toby
was alone and asleep and not drunk—Quill could
smell no liquor in the room. "Wake up," Quill said,
shaking him roughly.

"Wha'? Quill, what is it?" Toby sat up and ran
one hand through his spiky hair, thereby making it
look even worse. "Are you going to make a habit
of waking me all the time?"

"Perhaps, if you pull any more stunts like the
Drayton-Day thing," he snarled. "Get up. I need
you to go get her from Almack's and take her
home."

"Now? What time is it, man?"

"Only three, I believe."

"I have no carriage now! How will I get her?

204

The one I had earlier has been returned to the livery."

"You have your horse stabled nearby, don't you?" he said, his tone not helpful.

"Yes, I do." Toby struggled to rise. He looked more closely at Quill's face. "Oh, man, you look fit to kill me. I don't know what to do to make up for this whole affair."

Quill saw his sincerity, so he softened toward his old friend. "I am giving you the opportunity now. By tomorrow it will all be forgiven and forgotten, but tonight I cannot manage to go back for her. The past few days have taken their toll on me, and I'm bushed. I must go to my bed." He offered his hand to Toby. "I am truly exhausted."

Toby turned up the wick on the lamp near him, then examined Quill's face carefully. "You don't look too good. Do you want to doss down here?"

"No, I must return home, or the household will be sure I am lying dead somewhere in a dark alley. Ever since the Rutledge abduction of Diana, everyone is on pins and needles."

"I will dress and accompany you home, Quill. You look like death."

Quill shook his head. "No, I can manage. You have to go rescue Camilla. Let me sit for a minute, though." He slumped on a chair as Toby dressed rapidly.

Once he had finished dressing, Toby led the way downstairs. He looked over his shoulder from time to time. "Are you sure, Quill, that you can make it home?" He had to rouse the porter again. "Quickly—have my horse saddled."

Within minutes the stable boy had brought Toby's horse around, and left him next to Brutus, and the porter gave each of them a hand up. "Thanks," Toby said to the two men and flipped them each a few coppers. Once more he asked Quill, "Are you going to make it home?"

"Of course!" Quill shouted. "You're as bad as any female for fretting. Go on, man. Camilla has cooled her heels long enough."

Raising a hand to placate him, Toby said, "All right, all right. Don't get your drawers in a twist. I'm going." He turned the horse and said over his shoulder, "I'll call on you tomorrow. And Quill," he said hesitantly, "I am sorry about not taking Anna."

Once he was gone, Quill nudged Brutus on home. He could hardly wait to get inside and in bed. The cold, damp air seeped into his bones. He dozed a bit as Brutus stepped lightly on the cobbles.

Deciding to take a shortcut, through a warehouse district near the Two Swans, Quill reined the horse off the main thoroughfare. There was no light between the large, leaning, hulking buildings. He could smell rotting garbage and unwashed human flesh.

A rat scurried off to his left, causing Brutus to twist to the right. "Steady, Brutus," he said. He urged

Brutus to pick up his speed, but the horse jibbed at every shadow. His fatigue shortened his patience, even with Brutus. "Cut it out," he snapped.

Brutus snorted and shook his head, stopped and backed, pulled everything to avoid going forward. He tried to get his head to refuse Quill's directions.

Because he was fighting the horse, Quill didn't notice the three large shadows off to his left until they had grabbed his foot and tried to yank him out of the saddle. At that, Brutus reared and whinnied shrilly. Quill heard hooves strike the cobbles, then the dull thud of a hoof on flesh and the grunt of pain from one of his attackers.

He realized his fatigue had made him careless. And now thieves had waylaid him and wrecked his plans for a good night's sleep!

One of them whipped Brutus, who bolted. When Quill hit the ground, his attackers cudgeled his head, shoulders, and lower back. At that point Quill passed out.

The next morning Lucas Cranford was up and out of bed fairly early. He felt nearly normal, after days of illness. He couldn't remember the first two days after Wentworth's arrival, but he did remember the trip here to the Wentworths' house in London the day before in his carriage.

Schunk

He remembered that it had been Quill who took charge of getting him here; he remembered Quill's words, once he realized Lucas's illness was not just alcohol poisoning but also something contagious: "I cannot in good conscience leave you here alone while you are ill." That had transpired sometime in the haze of the first two days of illness.

At any rate, he appreciated Quill's conscience. He did not think he could have survived without Wentworth's aid. Without the friendship and concern that had inspired that aid, he wouldn't have cared enough to survive.

He dressed in a leisurely fashion. It felt immensely luxurious not to feel sick or, beleaguered by black demons. When he ambled downstairs to find the dining room, he took the liberty of enjoying the artwork on the walls of the halls, stairways, and foyer. Wentworth had excellent taste.

Sunlight streamed in through the crescent window above the heavy oak front door. He could feel his spirits lift, for the first time since that day nearly two years ago when he was left waiting at the altar for Diana to become his bride. He had felt personally, totally rejected, a laughingstock before family and friends. He had been sure she had turned against him, due to some tragic flaw in himself he didn't even know existed. Whatever anyone might have accused him of at the time, he would have accepted as truth.

He shook his head to clear it of the negatives

about to overwhelm him again. He would not fall prey to the demons again. There was hope, although difficult to achieve, for his and Diana's life together. He could not subject her to his megrims now they could be together again. He felt ashamed, like a weakling, for having succumbed for so long to those demons.

He entered the dining room to find it empty. He rang for Randall, who came immediately. "I'm late, I fear, for breakfast. May I find something to eat?"

"Oh, of course, my lord. We're all at sixes and sevens since the master did not come home last night." Randall seemed preoccupied, that paragon of butlerdom who never faced a social situation he could not manage; even his attire looked mussed. *He must have a deep affection for Quill*, Lucas thought. Aloud he said, "He was probably indisposed from last night's ball and spent the night at his club. Almack's was surely crowded."

Randall nodded. "That is possible. About your breakfast—I'll see to it right away. Please be seated."

The little man scurried out, and Lucas sat in one of the heavy carved chairs at the long table. He toyed with the sterling compote set on the table. Quill not here. He'd thought they would spend the morning making plans. Diana's court date was coming up soon. During his illness and drive to London, they hadn't discussed Quill's plans for the return to court. What had Wentworth decided for her defense?

Randall returned with a tray of foods, including Lucas's favorites, kippers, scrambled eggs, fresh bread, and marmelade. Randall poured him coffee, then said, "Will there be anything else?"

He shook his head no, then thanked Randall for serving him. As he ate, he thought about the coming days. He resolved to broach the subject as soon as Quill returned, to discover what plans Quill had made, and to take over the task himself if need be. Diana was the love of *his* life, not Quill's, so it was fitting he should plan her deliverance.

CHAPTER 19

Anna Kate slept late and awoke refreshed and ready to burst out in song. She got out of bed feeling as though she were floating on pale pink and periwinkle blue clouds. Quill had kissed her.

She finished her toilette, but did not dress beyond putting on an oversized white wool dressing gown. She did not want to enter into the quotidian nature of her usual schedule. She wanted to stay wrapped in fluff and dreams. She feared that if she dressed in her everyday clothes and left her room, she would lose the dreamy air she was breathing.

She even departed from her usual routine enough to ring for Susan. In the past she had not allowed herself to play the lady-of-the-manor role, servants at her beck and call. But today—today she would make an exception to that and every other rule.

Susan arrived and asked how her evening had gone. Anna Kate smiled at her so broadly that she figured she looked foolish. She didn't care.

"I am so glad, miss, that you had such a lovely time," Susan said, her voice warm with her affection for Anna. "It was a big evening for you."

Anna impulsively hugged Susan. "Oh, you can't guess how big! I'm in love, and I believe he loves me too!"

Susan returned her hug. "I'm happy for you."

"Have you recently seen your beau?" Anna asked, mindful of the fact that Susan did not have the liberty she had to go to a dance or other social gatherings with her beau.

Tears in her eyes, she shook her head. "He was supposed to come by this morning, but he didn't."

Anna covered Susan's hand with her own. "I'm so sorry. It's hard to wait and not know."

Susan nodded. "So hard." She lifted her head and smiled through her tears. "But don't fuss over me. You need your breakfast. I'll bring hot water, and then your tray."

"Are you sure you're fine? May I help in some way?"

"I'm fine," she said forcefully, then turned on her heel and left the room.

Oh, dear, Anna thought, *I've offended her.* She was too happy, however, to hold onto her regret, so she shrugged it off. She wrapped her arms around herself, snuggling into the large dressing gown, and began to waltz around the room.

Soon Susan brought her meal and hot water

for bathing. With a sigh Anna Kate accepted that she must give up her dreams for a while.

Besides, perhaps Quill would call. She was quite sure he would. After all, he had nearly declared for her last night.

She dressed slowly and deliberately in a new dress, in a delicious lavender. The nipped-in, high waist and the ribbons cascading down the front made her feel entirely feminine. She doubted that even Camilla Drayton-Day could make her feel out of pace with the *ton* today.

Once she had put on her kid slippers, she descended the stairs as regally as she could. It took tremendous will power, for she desired most of all to race down the steps so she could tell Constance all over again about dancing with Quill.

Once she reached the foyer, she hesitated by the silver tray for calling cards. Sifting through the few cards on the tray, Anna felt a pang of disappointment not to find her beloved's card among them. She told herself he surely had business to attend to, now that he was back in town after such a long absence. She could wait for him because they had a lifetime ahead of them.

By the end of that long, cold winter day, Anna Kate was fresh out of patience and forbearance. "If Quill were to walk in now, I would tear his hair out!" she exclaimed to Constance as they sat by the fire, Constance mending, Anna picking at her fingernails.

Maddeningly, Constance smiled benignly and said nothing. She merely continued to do her mending.

"Why hasn't he come to see me?" she wailed.

Carefully Constance put her mending down and gazed at Anna. "My dear," she said precisely, "I have no idea. I am sure that once you hear from him, he will tell you why, and it will be a good reason, at least from his view."

"You speak to me as though I were an idiot child," Anna said.

Constance's eyebrows shot up. "Perhaps that is because you sometimes act like one."

Anna arose, close to exploding in a huff.

Constance raised her hand to stop the explosion. "Anna Kate," she said sharply, "enough. If you speak what you are now thinking, you will have a fit of the megrims and later be overcome with guilt. So bridle your tongue!"

Eyes wide, brimming in tears, Anna swallowed, then spoke. "You are, as usual, perfectly right. Thank you." She sat back down on her chair and turned away to look at the fire, not at Constance. She did not speak again for perhaps ten minutes. It took her that long to gain her composure.

With a sigh of relief, thankful for the respite, Constance returned to her mending. Her usual gentle spirit at last calmed Anna's fiercely proud heart. Anna gulped down tears, then stood and crossed to Constance's side.

"Were you ever in Andover that time, about three years ago—my father was ill and had to have a locum in? It was Willard Mote—do you remember him?"

"Yes. He was a tall, stooping man, rather handsome, I thought, with that gray hair and the dark eyes."

"But brooding, right? Do you remember that?"

"Yes." She laughed. "I always thought he meant to marry you, but you laughed too often."

"Frivolous. That's what he called me."

"And?"

"I was thinking of his sermons that spring. The roses and hawthorns were in bloom, but he kept talking about how we needed to suffer. We didn't know what suffering was, living in England as we did, the mightiest power on earth."

"Yes?"

"Perhaps he's right. Do you think that's what's wrong with me? I just haven't suffered enough?"

Constance laughed. "You're working on your portion these days."

"But it isn't real suffering. He was talking about Peter's letters on suffering and his end, being crucified upside down. Terrible!"

Constance dropped her mending in her lap and stared at her. "Of course! And you want to suffer like that?"

Schunk

Anna clasped her hands under her chin and looked beatific. "But it would be good for my character, don't you think?"

Constance looked at her, then shook her head. "I'm sorry. I guess I'm missing something here. I thought at the time of those horrid sermons that he sounded so foolish."

"Why?"

"There are times we must suffer. I know our soldiers and sailors suffer. I know the poor suffer. I know full well that Diana has suffered."

"That's what I mean! And she looks so noble too!"

"Anna. Stop and think. Why would you want to suffer? Why not give thanks to the good Lord that you have food and a roof over your head, that you have clothing and good shoes to wear? I have never understood the vogue in being morose when we're adequately fed and clothed."

"I felt that way at the time, but then I thought I must be wrong. Perhaps Quill would like me better if I suffered."

"Oh, enough, Anna! You are a good, kind person, and you do what you can to help people. If your needs weren't adequately taken care of, how could you find the time or energy to help? Or Quill? He can do what he does only because he's a lord, with considerable income, and time—and good health—at his disposal! See reason here!"

Anna stopped pacing and looked at her. "You're

right, you're absolutely right."

Constance smiled roguishly. "Why, thank you, dear heart. You always were reasonable."

"Do you have some mending I can do? I'm good at darning socks."

Constance laughed, her voice sweet and high like a sleigh bell. "You can do all the socks! I detest them—my mother always said I put lumps in the darn."

Anna smiled widely. "Well," she said, "something I can do better than you can. This will be the first and only instance." She gathered up black stockings in small sizes to darn. "I see they're mostly Mary's."

"Yes," Constance said with a sigh, "she is very hard on her clothes."

"I always was too. That must be why she and I get along so well. I was quite hoydenish, you know."

Constance looked up at her under long lashes. "I would never have guessed..."

"Now, now. I was always told, over and over by Aunt Lydia, that irony does not become a lady."

Before Constance could continue the banter, the butler came in and said, "My lady, you have a caller."

"Quill!" Anna said.

"Quill?" he asked. "Oh, no, not at all."

"No? Oh, I will never survive learning to wait patiently, not ever."

The guest was someone Anna didn't know. After spending a few moments in polite interchange with the lady, a Lady Stanhope, she took the darning and excused herself. Once upstairs in her room, she closed the door behind her and leaned back against it, her hands full of stockings. She sighed. Would she spend the rest of her life waiting on his lordship's good pleasure? Somehow she imagined she would.

She also imagined it would be worth it for the times in between when he held her and kissed her.

On that thought she resolved to stop fretting about Quillen Rossiter's absence and to keep herself busy at useful tasks. She doubted she could stand her own company if she didn't keep occupied.

Once she'd finished the darning, she planned the next day: up at a decent hour, breakfast with the children, an outing with the pony, then back home to her letter writing. Then perhaps she would begin reading that book she had checked out from the lending library, *Pride and Prejudice*, by a Jane Austen. For years the author's name was a secret, but she had heard Miss Jane Austen's brother couldn't keep the secret any longer. Now it was a byword in the town.

She wondered if she would get more respect from people if she were a famous authoress. Quill wouldn't leave her cooling her heels all day if she were important!

"Now, none of that," she said to her reflection in the mirror. "This poor-me-ing gets you nowhere."

With that she began her nightly routine, removing the dress she had so carefully chosen that morning in hopes of Quill's seeing it, and hanging it up. At that point she remembered the pouch Diana had given her. Where had she put it? She supposed she ought to check on it, see that it was still safe. For all her blithe ignorance of the pouch, it could have disappeared!

She checked in the back of the wardrobe, where she kept a small box of her reticules. There, in the bottom of the box, was the rose reticule she'd carried that day, and in it was the pouch. She picked it up, felt it, hefted it, examined it. Quite dangerous for so unassuming an object.

She could only hope it didn't mean the death of her friend. She put it back with a final pat, for safety.

She returned to her nighttime routine, ended by washing her face and settling down to her prayers. "Dear Lord," she whispered, "please keep Diana—and Quill too—safe. I pray that Diana's healing continues, and that she is soon out from under Rutledge's hand. And dear Lord, help me be what I should be, instead of the whiny, babyish thing I am right now. I make myself and everyone else sick to death."

Late Thursday evening, as they sipped coffee in the

drawing room, Eleanor Wentworth gazed at Lucas Cranford, who was paying slim attention to a chess board by the fireplace. He and Quill had played chess this way as boys, one making his move, the other coming later to consider the next play.

Toby had been by an hour earlier to speak with Quill. His surprise that Quill hadn't returned home increased Lady Wentworth's alarm. Lucas in turn felt alarm for her. Her face looked pinched, and the skin around her mouth was tinged with blue.

"I think something is terribly wrong with my son." Her ravaged face tore at his heart. "I cannot believe he would have stayed at his club all day, with no word to me."

Lucas said nothing. He knew young men: few of Quill's age and rank cleared their calendars with their mothers!

She began picking at the crumpled handkerchief in her lap. She rose from her chair and crossed to the bell pull. "I will have Randall organize a search for him."

When the butler entered, Lucas saw that he too was suffering undue worry over Quill's absence. "Milady?" he asked.

"Please get Coachman John and the footman, and whoever else they can round up, to begin a search for Lord Wentworth."

Randall's face cleared. "Yes, milady. That will be so much better than merely worrying."

"Tell John to find Sir Toby first. He may give

us some leads on his whereabouts." She began pacing and wringing her hands. "I cannot believe I didn't question Toby more closely earlier. We have lost hours of searching for him, as well as the daylight."

Lucas arose from the sofa by the chessboard. He came to her and offered his hand. When she put her thin-as-china hand in his, he pressed it gently. "You need your rest. I will help by going to find Toby. Randall can man the house, in case Quill comes in or in case John returns with any news. I will not tell you not to worry. But hold firm; we will find him." He turned on his heel and exited the room.

Seconds after, John entered the room, hat in his hands. "My lady, Brutus has just returned to the stable. He has been tied with a rope around his neck—I can see the burns on his flesh—and he has been whipped. It's possible he was stolen by thieves and Lord Wentworth is all right."

Eleanor Wentworth's icy cold hands flew to her face, and she gasped for air. Quill was not all right, he was not.

Quill's fever had run high all day Thursday. At dusk it fell, and he could begin to think.

He looked around him. He was in one of the warehouses near the Two Swans, he felt sure. He frowned. Where was Brutus? He'd realized, hours earlier, that the horse had been tied to an iron ring set in the wall nearby. Ah, yes, there were droppings over there.

He was bound, his hands fortunately before him. He ached enough, but how much worse the pain would be if his captors had tied them behind him.

They had taken his money, but robbery hadn't been their purpose. He'd heard the three talking, about the broken leg one of them had suffered when Brutus had struck him with a hoof, about the money they'd be paid for his disappearance. He'd been abducted, to be sure he couldn't accomplish something—what, he didn't know.

Then, just before sunrise they'd slipped out. They hadn't returned all day. He had no food, no water, which he couldn't have consumed anyway, with his hands tied. They had left him there to die. But he didn't want to die, he wanted to marry Anna Kate.

Anna Kate. He tried to picture how she'd looked at Almack's when she'd approached him after his excoriation of Toby. Lovely, lovely.

Thinking made him tired. He closed his eyes to rest them.

As the night wore on, his condition worsened. He lay on the cold floor of the warehouse. From time to time, he thought he could hear someone calling him, but he wasn't sure.

Death in Exile

Hours later, he awoke to hear a large wooden door being drawn open. Weak sunlight sent a shaft of brilliance through the interior of the abandoned building. He lifted his head, to see who it was. Had his attackers returned, to finish the job?

"Lord Wentworth!" a familiar voice gasped. "Is it you?"

"John?" His voice croaked, unaccustomed to speech.

"Brutus brought me here, milord. He knew where you were."

Quill attempted a smile. He felt the skin on his lips crack. "Good boy," he whispered.

John led Brutus into the warehouse and over to where Quill lay. The horse ducked his head to sniff at Quill's hair. It tickled.

"Good boy," he repeated. He felt cold hands fumble with the ropes on his hands. When they fell away, the blood rushed to his hands, and he thought he would scream with pain. "Slow, man—go easy." When John untied his feet, he took a deep breath, but they weren't as painful as his hands, which he flexed and then opened and and shut to clench his fists. It hurt, but he gritted his teeth.

Then he licked his parched lips. "Say—can I have some water?"

"As soon as we get you home."

John and Brutus got him back to Wentworth Place by the time the sun had fully risen. "Take me to the kitchen door," he croaked. "It would spread gossip for all the neighbors to see me come home like this—they'd think I was drunk and had been in a fight."

"Yes, my lord," John said, willing to do anything his master asked of him.

"What day is it?" he asked once they had reached the back of the house.

John helped him down from the horse. "Friday, my lord."

"Friday! But I was supposed to go offer for Anna—yesterday!" He struggled to stand. His legs gave way under him. John lifted him, placing Quill's right arm around his neck, then his own arm around Quill's chest; at that point Quill passed out.

"Oof, you're heavy, my lord," he gasped, aware, however, that Quill could not hear.

Cook met them at the door as John was carrying him inside. "Get Randall and the footman. And anyone else, except her ladyship. He's in a bad way."

"I'm here, John," Lady Wentworth said. "You've found him." John looked at her. In spite of lost sleep, her face was radiant. "Bring him in. We will lay him out in the kitchen by the fire and see what he needs. Besides a bath and clean clothes," she said, smiling as she ran one hand over his shoulder. Lucas came in then, tucking his shirt into his trousers as he entered. "He's home, Lucas. We can get him well. You'll see."

The calm in her voice made John wonder if she had lost her mind. But he soon knew better as she organized the bath, the fetching of clean clothes, the making of broth with lots of ginger and beef stock.

He excused himself to go take care of Brutus's wounds. That horse deserved an extra scoop of oats this morning.

Within the hour, they had Quill cleaned up and put into bed upstairs. He had some fever but it wasn't bad, so he was resting fairly calmly.

Lady Wentworth sent a footman to get Mr. Sumner in to see him. She did not want their regular physician; the word that Quill had been attacked would spread through all their friends, and her proud young lord would not like that.

Mme Vero sent back word that he couldn't come, he was still recovering from a beating. Lady Wentworth knew nothing of that, but she wondered at the wide occurrence of beatings these days.

Nevertheless, Blaine Sumner arrived soon after. The disheveled little surgeon looked more kempt than she'd ever seen him, but he was pale and drawn.

She watched anxiously over his shoulder as he checked her son over. He looked almost cheerful once he'd completed his examination and pronounced him likely to survive. "But he needs to quit hanging about with such rough sorts."

"You are well?" she asked.

"Yes, my lady. Veronique and I are to be wed in a fortnight."

"Congratulations. I must send her my best wishes. But what of the beating you received?"

He glanced over his shoulder at Quill on the bed. "Oh, a case of mistaken identity, I believe."

Once he left, worry descended on the household again.

Later that day, when Quill's fever had broken and he'd begun to rest easier, Lucas told Lady Wentworth to go rest. "You need to eat, to rest. I will stay with him. I'll even spoon that evil-looking broth down him."

He stayed with him for hours. From time to time, Randall or Mrs. Godwin, both with heavy steps and bowed shoulders, came to check on them, to spell him at dinnertime. It was one of the longest days Lucas had ever lived through, nearly as long as those days after Diana's disappearance before their wedding. It all felt too much like the same senseless sort of suffering, with too much asking of questions with no answers. Why? Who? Then why again.

Lady Wentworth spent the long evening with Quill. Lucas stayed with her, with only brief forays out of the room for coffee or a walk down the street, to clear his head. At midnight he sent her to bed. "You must rest, Lady Wentworth. Quill will blame me if you fall ill." Besides, he had questions to ask, and Lady Wentworth would not approve his waking Quill just to get some silly questions answered.

Once she was gone, he grasped Quill's shoulder and shook him lightly. "Quill, can you speak to me?"

Quill opened his eyes and focused on Lucas. "What?"

"Can you tell me what happened? Who did this?"

Quill's face sharpened. "Brutus! How is he? They beat him, you know. He broke one of the wretches' leg." He laughed without humor. "I wish he'd killed him."

"Brutus is fine. John dressed his wounds and now has taken over cosseting and spoiling him. He tells us what a splendid animal the creature is." He paused, then asked, "Quill, what have you planned about getting Diana back to London? Her trial is coming up."

With his eyes tight shut, he scowled. "Diana. Yes, court. She's safe right now."

"What have you planned? I need to know, so I can carry it out."

Quill shook his head, and it rolled back and forth on his crumpled pillow. "I can't remember."

"All right. Don't push yourself. There's still time."

Quill visibly relaxed. Then his eyes flew open. "Anna Kate! Where is Anna?"

Startled, Lucas nearly dropped the bowl of

broth he'd been feeding Quill. "Anna? She was with you?"

"Yes." Quill nodded, then frowned. "My head..."

"She was with you when you were attacked?"

Quill was becoming agitated. "Attacked? No, she wasn't attacked. She was dancing and kissing...kissing me. Then I sent her home. How would she get attacked? I'm sure Toby and Dunstable..."

Lucas patted Quill's shoulder. "She's surely fine. I'll go check on her in the morning."

"Please." Quill subsided, and within moments, he was asleep.

Now a little after two in the morning, Lucas fell into despair. His black demons told him many more would suffer because of his inadequacies. He knew nothing, not even who was behind the attack on Quill. To ease a growing headache, he poured himself a large measure of brandy, to shut up the demons' voices, but as he lifted the fat-bowled crystal glass to his mouth, he recalled the state Quill had found him in, at least partially due to his previous brandy consumption. The depression he suffered would be worsened, not relieved, by the brandy.

He lowered the glass and gazed at the fine cognac in it, then heaved it with all his might across the room, where it shattered in the fireplace. The flames danced high in yellows and blues when the alcohol hit. He made a fist and jammed it into the thick plastered wall of the room. The pain and the telltale crunch satisfied him; now he no longer needed to suffer.

But he had to put all his failings behind him. He had to check on Anna and plan for Diana's return to London.

Lucas got up and quietly left the room. A footman stood outside the door. "Go fetch Randall or Mrs. Godwin. I must sleep."

"Yes, milord." The footman bowed slightly, then left.

"Then in the morning I'll go see if Anna is safe at home. All this has the earmarks of Rutledge's tactics." He strode down the hall to his room. "Thank God Diana is safe."

At about nine on Saturday morning Quill's fever broke. With the reduction of fever came the spiking of his temper. "What do you people mean, keeping me in bed like this?" he roared when Randall and Mrs. Godwin came in to bathe him, change the bedding, and spell Lady Wentworth in the task of spooning broth into his mouth.

Lady Wentworth began to laugh; in her fatigue she laughed so hard that she crossed the boundary to hysteria and was soon also crying, in gratitude to have her sorehead son back again. "I have never in my life been so glad to hear you roar!" She leaned over him and placed a kiss on his cheek. "You can yell all you want; it is like the music of the spheres to me."

At that he snorted and crossed his arms over his chest and looked as sullen as ever. But she thought she detected a softening of his fury.

"You've been most diligent in caring for me, Mother, and I thank you." His tone held a hint of repentance.

"You're welcome. Lucas helped too. I do wonder, however, if I should ask Anna Kate for the receipt for that soup she brought Diana."

"Anna Kate!" he said. "Oh, no!"

"What?" she asked, alarmed.

"Have you gotten word to her that I've been wounded? She will be awaiting my arrival to pay my respects today."

"Today?"

"Yes, after the assembly at Almack's last night..."

"Last night! You have lost two days. This is Saturday, Quill."

"Two days!" With that bit of news, he flung the covers back, nearly knocking Mrs. Godwin over in his haste. He grimaced in pain. "She'll be sure I am neglecting her. I nearly declared for her at Almack's. And that Drayton-Day fiasco—she will be sure Camilla has ruined her reputation. I must get dressed. Will you women get out of my room?"

"Quill, mind your manners. You are not going anywhere," Eleanor said. "You get right back in that bed."

At that point Lucas stepped into the room. "I do hope you will forgive my eavesdropping, but I heard you outside the room. I wanted you to know something."

"Cranford." Quill hesitated, thinking about what his next steps should be. "What is it?"

"Your coachman found the man with the broken leg. He's been arrested, but not before he told John, with perhaps overly zealous encouragement, that Rutledge had hired him and his chums."

"Rutledge. Of course."

"And I also need to know what your plans are in relation to Diana's court case. I will carry your commands out while you recuperate."

Quill looked at him, the wheels almost visibly turning in his head as he considered Lucas's words. "All right," he said at last. "That may be the best idea." He continued his perusal of Lucas's face. "You look almost human. Your megrims gone?"

Lucas flushed. "Yes, Quill, I do believe they are, at least for today. I'd like to return you a favor now, though, to repay your kindness to me. May I deliver a message to Anna?"

"Right. You all please go on out so I can think about a note to Anna. Randall, will you come back in about ten minutes?"

"Yes, milord. But do you need writing paper?"

He glanced around the room. "Of course. See to it, man."

Randall exchanged a look with Eleanor, then hid a grin. His master was getting better. She returned his smile.

Out in the hall she suddenly felt her great exhaustion. She weaved a bit, and Lucas stepped up to offer his arm. "May I help you, my lady?"

She put one hand on his arm, the other to her head. "I do feel quite queer."

He glanced back at Mrs. Godwin, who bustled up to take charge. "My lady, let us go to your room. I will order some tea for you, and perhaps some of that good broth."

"The broth," Eleanor said. "I need Anna's receipt for it."

"Yes, my lady," Mrs. Godwin said. "We will send for it right away."

"I'm going soon," Lucas said, "with a note for her. I can get the receipt then."

"Thank you," Eleanor said weakly.

Once the two of them got Lady Wentworth to her room, Mrs. Godwin shooed Lucas away. "Go for that receipt as soon as you can manage," she said.

He nodded and left the room.

"Do you think you are ill, milady?" the housekeeper asked Eleanor.

"I...I don't know. I feel so odd."

Within moments, Mrs. Godwin had Lady

Wentworth's shoes off and her feet up on a has-
sock. A maid arrived soon after with a cup of steaming tea and honey. "Take your medicine and drink
this. If you are merely tired, this tea will tell us so,"
Mrs. Godwin said briskly, to hide her worry.

Chapter 20

Anna Kate dressed Saturday morning in the rose carriage dress she had worn the first day she saw Quill in town. It wasn't quite as fine as the lavender one she'd worn two days before, but it would do. She kept to her plans for most of the morning, but by lunchtime, she was beside herself. She wished she could take up swearing and kicking the furniture.

At tea, she said to Constance, "I believe I need to start a school. I am too directive for this passive lady's life. It will never work. No man will ever tolerate my temper or my detestation of sitting and doing nothing."

Constance looked at her. "You may be right, about the school, I mean. You are very good with children. I don't know whether any man will tolerate you. That remains to be seen." She frowned, then took a sip of her tea. "But I don't believe Mother Stanfield or Lady Wentworth will forget their goal to bring you out."

Anna rose from her chair by the tea table, which was set in front of the fire, and began to walk about the room. "Perhaps if I go home and don't return..."

"They will never allow it. Sit down, Anna Kate, you give me a crook in my neck from watching you. You need some activity to enthrall you, that I do believe. What about Diana's plight? Isn't court fast approaching?"

"I believe so, but Quill is in charge, so I am left out in the cold on that too."

The two stared disconsolately into the fire. Soon the butler entered the room and said, "Lord Breckin, my lady, for Miss Forsythe."

Anna jumped up from her chair. "Lucas!" she said. "Perhaps he has some news for me. Anything to end this horrible ennui."

Lucas entered. His face, still gaunt, showed the ravages of his drinking and illness, although the bruises from Rutledge's beating had healed.

Anna gasped. "Lucas! Are you all right? You look like death." She went forward to take his hands.

He bowed slightly. "Thank you for your concern. I'm much better. I was quite ill, but Lord Wentworth helped me regain my health."

Anna lifted her hands, clasped as though in prayer, up to her lips. "Quill?" she repeated weakly.

"He found me in Kent near death. As you know, he brought me here and made it to Almack's for your dance just in time."

She nodded, eyes wide.

"Since then he has been quite sick himself."

"Sick?"

"I reproach myself. I was suffering my private demons." He stopped himself. "This will not be easy for you to hear, but Quill was attacked by thieves."

"Thieves! Oh, no! How is he? Did they...?"

"He is alive, and I do believe he is on the mend. He bellowed at everyone this morning." Belatedly he made note of Constance's presence in the room. "Lady Cadogen," he said, bowing over her hand.

"May I offer you tea?" she asked, never one to forget the amenities.

"Yes, thank you." He did not sit, for Anna was still standing.

At last, Constance said, "Won't you both be seated? I cannot serve the tea with my head craned back to look at you." Her voice was light, with no hint of reproach.

Anna quickly sat, then picked up her cup for a sip. Lucas followed her lead and said, "This tea is perfect. It is beastly cold out today."

Anna did not speak. She feared she might frighten him off, the only line to Quill she had at the moment.

After he ate three small cakes, Lucas closed his eyes in appreciation. "You serve a beautiful tea, my lady," he said to Constance.

Anna thought she would scream. Why was he dragging this out?

As though reading her thoughts, he said, "Quill has sent a letter for you, Anna Kate. He regrets his tardiness in letting you know of his condition." He handed her a folded piece of vellum, sealed with wax and Quill's signet.

She took it from him almost reverently and held it close to her nose. Perhaps she could smell his bay rum after-shave on it. At last she opened it. She read silently, then looked up, a beatific smile transforming her face. "He'll come as soon as he is able." She did not share anything more from the letter, but Lucas at least knew it contained much more than this small snippet of news.

He grinned. "He misses you too, I am confident, Anna. My best wishes for you both. I have another duty to perform: Lady Wentworth desires your receipt for the soup you prepared for Diana those long weeks ago. She may be sickening too. She is at least extremely fatigued."

"Oh!" Anna popped up again, like a jack in the box. "I can take it to the Wentworths and make it myself while there. I would love to be of service," she pleaded, to Constance.

Constance nodded. "You may go, if Lord Breckin will accompany you."

"Of course, my lady."

Anna waited for not another word. She spun around and flitted out of the room.

Lucas and Constance shared a smile. "She is much in love, is she not?" he asked.

"Much."

"I know Quill feels a strong duty for her, just as he does in a different way for Diana."

Alarmed, Constance spoke rapidly. "Then he doesn't love her, but merely feels a duty to her? She must not pursue her affection for him if he has no love for her."

"I did not mean to imply that. He does love her. But these other obligations, beginning with Diana, pull at him. I hope to step into the gap for Diana's honor. I love her, you know."

"Yes, I know."

"I have spent too much time feeling sorry for myself. It's time to give all that up and go forward."

Anna soon reappeared, wearing her cloak and clutching the receipt in her hand. "Let's go, Lucas. There's no time to lose."

CHAPTER 21

Anna Kate climbed happily into the Wentworth landau that Lucas had brought. He handed her in, then the basket of makings for her special broth the cook had passed to him, and sat across from her. She felt so joyous she wanted to sing. "Would you take it amiss if I were to burst into song?" she teased.

"That depends on how well you sing."

"Not that well. Don't you remember how Papa despaired of my voice?" She smiled, so filled with happiness that even the memory of her sad attempts to sing could not dampen it.

"You may certainly go ahead and sing. It will not offend me. I won't mind a few missed notes."

She laughed but did not sing. "He is better, you say."

"I'd say so. He went from raging fever to ranting temper in only a few moments earlier today. He is as cross as ever, so his mother assures us all he is quite well. I'm worried about her, however. I pray her incapacity today was due to fatigue and not illness."

"I do too."

They arrived at Wentworth House, and Lucas accompanied her into the house, carrying her basket for her. "I'll leave you here. I have another errand to run for Quill." There was a sense of deep satisfaction in him.

"About Diana?"

He nodded. "Yes, but I can't burden you with the knowledge of what that is. I do opine this ordeal will soon end, happily." He took her hands in his. "Pray for us, Anna. I remember how much you prayed when a child. Praying well may be better than singing well." With those words he kissed her cheek and was gone.

Anna waited patiently—she complimented herself on the fact—until Mrs. Godwin came to greet her. "I dare say you would like to see Lord Wentworth."

"Yes, may I?" Her heart was beating fast, and she realized her palms were moist. So unladylike, she knew, but then her heart did not care, nor did her palms for that matter.

Trying to proceed in as stately a fashion as possible, Anna held her skirts up as they ascended the stairs so she wouldn't embarrass herself by tripping. Surely she had never felt such excitement as she did now, on her way to visit a man just up from his sick bed. If they married, she would have years of visiting him in his private quarters. That thought made her blush. Surely she was the veriest hussy!

Mrs. Godwin waved her into his room. His mother was sitting on a *chaise longue*, her feet wrapped in woolen blankets and a mug of hot tea in her hands. She looked flushed, but otherwise well.

"My lady," Anna said with a curtsy, "you look well. I had feared to find you ill."

"No, just very tired. It is good to see you, my dear. You look lovely."

Again Anna blushed, then whispered, "Thank you, my lady." She feared to glance at Quill; his visage would bring her to the edge of her strength, so much did she love him.

"Yes, Anna, you do," he said softly.

She raised her eyes to him. Leaning against the mantel, his lean body clad in tight breeches and a navy coat over a yellow waistcoat and well-layered cravat, he looked the perfect gentleman to her. His eyes and mouth were soft, his cheeks a trifle sunken. He had several cuts and bruises around his eyes, but otherwise he looked fine. The angry Quill was not before her today, only a gentle one, as glad to see her as she was to see him.

She curtsied again to him. "My lord." She looked deep into his eyes. Oh, how she wished she could run to him. "I was saddened to hear of the attack."

He laughed. "So was I! When I learned I had

lost two days, I was enraged that I had failed in my courtesy call to you. You were very lovely at Almack's. Mother—" he gestured toward his mother with his head— "has heard from some of her relations that you were the loveliest thing there."

"Oh, surely not," she said without thinking.

"Do not contradict," he said, a teasing tone in his voice. "You were quite the most beautiful young woman there."

"Thank you, my lord," she said with another brief curtsy. She was blushing again, or was it still? "You are very kind."

Eleanor reached a hand out to her. "Come close, my dear. We are remiss in our manners, keeping you standing this way."

Quill moved a chair close to his mother's chaise.

Once she sat beside Eleanor, she found her tongue. "I have brought the ingredients for that broth, my lady. I believe your cook is putting it together for you now."

"Thank you." She patted Anna's hand.

Quill cleared his throat, then spoke. "Anna, we have a proposal to make to you."

She looked questioningly at them both. This would not be a wedding proposal, not this way.

"For the time being, I must pretend a romantic interest in Camilla."

Horrified, she nearly fainted. "No."

"It is only for a short time," Eleanor beguiled her. "You will see. It is necessary for Diana's court appearance next week."

Anna shook her head. She felt her spirits defeated. She had hoped to be able to shout her love for Quill from the rooftops. Even more, she wanted him to shout out his.

Quill spoke again. "The worst thing is that I must ask you to spend an evening in the company of that Drayton-Day creature."

"What? Here? At a party?" With that she rose so abruptly the chair fell over behind her. "I cannot..."

"She is spreading tales that you are my paramour."

"What?" she shouted.

Quill crossed to her side and took her hands in his. "Please hear us out."

Eleanor nodded to encourage Anna to listen.

"There is no possible way I could tolerate being in her company, especially not if she is saying such things! What would my father say? He would be stricken!"

Quill drew her into his arms, forgetful, it seemed, of his mother's presence. "Hush, Anna. Let me finish."

She struggled to get away from him. "No! This would humiliate him so."

"Listen!" he snapped, holding her even tighter.

She gave up struggling and began to sob. Eleanor arose and patted her on the back. "I will be back in a few moments."

Schunk

"Wait!" Anna said as Eleanor stepped out of the room.

"My mother has always been the soul of propriety. And here she is leaving a young miss alone in my presence, in my arms!" He leaned down and kissed her very tenderly on the lips.

"Quill," she whispered.

He kissed her again, and she returned his kiss, passionately. She felt herself melting into his arms as he continued to hold her close.

At last he pulled back a half-step, somewhat flushed. His eyes sparkled. "Well, I must not continue this, at least not yet." He lay his hand against her cheek. "You are so lovely, sweet Anna."

"I am not the least bit sweet, my lord. That you must know." She knew she should remove herself from his arms now that he had loosened his hold on her.

"Bittersweet perhaps, like dark chocolate." He moved in again for another kiss.

She felt all her reticence dissolving as she returned his kiss with growing ardor. Oh, how she loved him.

She then realized: he hadn't told her that he loved her. What was his plan? "But why the subterfuge, Quill?" she asked now, pulling away from him. Her reason was reasserting itself. "I don't understand. It seems an unnecessarily complicated ploy."

"I don't believe anything else will suffice. She is a cousin to Rutledge."

"You don't mean it."

"She has plotted with him to trap me in matrimony with her. In order to protect Diana—and you, if she is bandying about your name in such a shameless manner—I must pretend a romantic interest in her. If she besmirches your name or mine, or Lucas's, it will play hob with our vouching for Diana in court. Since Rutledge killed Mathers—"

Anna Kate shook her head. "No, he didn't!"

He turned to stare at her. "What?"

She covered her mouth with her hand. "I..."

He grabbed her and squeezed her arms so hard she flinched. "You're hurting me."

He lessened the force of his grasp but didn't let her go. "Tell me what you know." He shook her a little, his eyes so fierce she wished she could hide in a hole. "This is very important, Anna. You can't keep a secret from me. What do you know?"

Tears sprung hot to her eyes. "Oh, don't, Quill. You'll make me cry, and you hate that!"

He took a deep breath and deliberately slowed his speech. "This is a matter of life and death, Anna Kate. You have to tell me."

"But he's so evil. Does it matter if you think he's guilty of one more crime?"

"You know it does." His eyes bored into her as he waited for her to speak.

"Well, it was like this." And she told him all about her outing on the pony cart, pretending she was another Miss Merrill. "He seemed innocent of the murder, but surely the other man knew something. And they didn't notice me, until the end. And then I still played dumb and turned around very slowly to make me way back to the house."

He'd blanched by the time she got to the part of eavesdropping on Rutledge's conversation. Then he took himself over to the chaise his mother had vacated and let himself slowly sink into it. "He could have killed you. He probably recognized you and is plotting to kill you now."

"Oh, no," she said blithely, "I'm sure not. I was fairly well disguised."

He let his glance rove over her figure and face. "I doubt that. I don't think you could succeed in hiding your face and form."

She blushed and decided not to pursue that line of thought.

Quill rubbed his face, fatigue evident in the slump of his shoulders, the grayness of his skin. "This changes things. What does this mean for our plan to bring Diana back?"

Anna kept quiet, wisely, she thought, while he ruminated over the ramifications of this new development.

At last he roused himself, stood up, and began to pace. "Who was this slim, elegant man?"

"I don't know, Quill. The other man was of course the one with the bushy beard I saw that day at your house."

He nodded. "All right," he said, taking her back

in his arms. "I don't know what all this means, but it doesn't seem to indicate our original plan is unsound. Just promise me you won't do such a thing again. If it gets out..." He ran his fingers through his hair, mussing it much as Toby habitually did.

"Well, back to the plans for the party. While I distract Drayton-Day, Lucas will retrieve Diana from Kent. The fact that Rutledge didn't kill Mathers doesn't relieve him of the guilt for nearly killing Diana." He let her go now and began to pace. She wondered if he had forgotten her presence in his preoccupation with Rutledge's perfidy. He now turned back to her, his eyes gleaming with purpose. "It will be over soon, I promise. Then, if you will have me, I shall declare for you."

She felt a *frisson* of fear. Right now this plan of Quill's seemed more dangerous than prudent. "Oh, Quill," she said as she walked back into his arms. "What if Rutledge learns of this plot? He will kill you." Tears rose in her eyes, for fear of what she might lose.

He gripped her upper arms with his full strength. She squirmed in discomfort. "He may try but he won't succeed. He didn't this time."

"Rutledge did this?"

"I'm sure of it. Remember this." He crushed her against him and kissed her one last time, with all the power and passion he had. "I will come back to you, Anna Kate Forsythe. Do not forget."

CHAPTER 22

The next two days had to be the longest of Anna's life. She often thought she had suffered before, but nothing approached the agony she was in.

Once having been in Quill's arms and tasted his strength and passion if only briefly, she now felt as though her arm or her hand or her heart had been ripped from her body. The ache filled her whole mind.

The time for the Wentworths' party was approaching. She dreaded the whole idea but could not discuss it with anyone.

Constance came into her room while Susan was dressing Anna's hair. "I feel as though you are grieving. Can you not tell me what is on your heart?"

Tears in her eyes, Anna shook her head. "It is nothing, Constance. You know how changeable my emotions are. This is temporary; I will soon be merry again."

Constance found Anna's eyes in the mirror. "If

you say so. I'll pray for you."

The words tore at Anna's wounded heart. "Oh, Constance, thank you. That will mean the world to me." She forced a smile for her friend. "I'll be myself again soon. Please retain your never-ending patience with me, I beseech you."

Still disturbed, Constance could not clear the concern from her face, but she said, "I will, I promise." Then she left the room.

Anna felt she had betrayed Constance's loyalty, but she could not share her secret, not yet. How many days until she could?

Soon she was dressed in a Nile green satin gown. It revealed her creamy white shoulders a bit too much for her comfort, but also brought out the highlights in her hair and made her eyes look green. *But not as green as Camilla's*, she reminded herself. *How will I face that little witch? How can I face anyone tonight, with the gossip spreading I am Quill's paramour? Will this ploy stem the gossip?*

She didn't know. While Quill assured her it would, she couldn't believe it. A lady's reputation was made or broken in salons where gossip flowed like wine, staining those it touched.

And the most painful part of it was that she could not take shelter in Quill's arms. He would be fawning on Camilla, and she knew her tattered heart would break.

Susan placed her hand on Anna's shoulder. "I don't know," she said softly, "what you are going through, but you are fine and strong, and you will come out on the other side fine and strong."

"Oh, Susan," Anna said as she burst into tears. She turned and threw herself into the maid's arms. "I am so frightened."

Susan didn't speak, but she patted Anna affectionately.

Anna bit her lip to stop the tears. "You're right. I am strong. I can stand and face them all on my own, because I'm my father's daughter. And—" here she broke off, before speaking Quill's name— "he will be proud." Susan would think she meant her father, but it was Quill she wanted to please now.

Susan placed cold cloths on Anna's eyes to reduce the swelling. "Sometimes cold tea is good for swelling," she said.

"There are some dregs in my cup over on the tray."

Quietly Susan continued to place compresses on Anna's eyes. At last she said, "There. Now no one will guess."

"That I have been crying my eyes out," Anna added ruefully. "Some day I will quit crying, forever."

"Don't say it. You do not want a heart so cold it never weeps."

Lucas arrived at ten PM. Anna was so weary from

her emotional outburst that she wanted to beg off, but she knew she could not. Lucas looked as glum as she felt. Wordlessly, he helped her into Constance's ermine cape.

Constance's brow was furrowed, but she did not question Anna. "Have a good time," she said.

Anna knew just how hollow the wish was; Constance guessed she couldn't anticipate a good time. "Thank you," she said quietly.

Lucas was silent, distanced in his own thoughts. She did not try to make conversation; no topics appealed. She wondered about his proposed trip to bring Diana back to town, but she didn't want to ask him.

Many carriages arranged themselves around the Wentworths' front steps, some coming, some leaving, some discharging their passengers. Never had Anna seen such sumptuous trappings as were displayed tonight, not even on the Wednesday night at Almack's.

She noted a black lacquer coach with the Prince Regent's emblem on the side. He was present tonight to see her shamed also?

He was a gambling crony of Rutledge's and surely here to bless the romantic involvement between Lord Wentworth and Camilla Drayton-Day, Rutledge's kin. Was his presence here a bribe to silence Quill in the affair of Rutledge's thieving wife?

Anna's stomach tightened. She was glad she had eaten little for supper. She would have lost it for sure, thanks to her attack of nerves.

She entered as regally as she could manage, her hand on Lucas's arm, her head held high. She remembered Quill's words at Almack's, about her regrettable tendency to hold her nose too high. Tonight she intended to hold it as high as possible. She would need to, in order to avoid catching the eye of anyone who might sneer at such a jumped-up miss.

Never had she felt so exposed, so stared and glared at. She wished she could reclaim her cape and wrap herself in it for protection. At least Lucas hadn't left her side—yet. He would before the night was over, of that fact she was sure.

Aware of a commotion on one side of the drawing room, she asked Lucas to accompany her to the punch table not far from a swelling knot of people.

"It is the Prince," he whispered in her ear.

"If I have to suffer this party, I may as well get a glimpse of him. I may never have another chance."

Lucas shook his head in amusement at her. "Of course, you will." He led her through the throng of people, introducing her as he went. "You certainly make any man proud to have you on his arm, Anna."

"You are kind."

Once they got close enough to the side of the room, Anna could see a tall man with a big head of blond, curly hair. She recognized him from pictures in the papers. He was fair and somewhat handsome, although bloated from his dissipated life.

Close up, she could see the telltale broken blood vessels reddening his nose and cheeks, the sure sign of his excesses in drinking and eating. He didn't look healthy.

A wave of pity washed over her, shocking her with its force. Pity for the Prince Regent, the most important man in the most important city in the most important nation in the world? It made no sense, but pity she did feel for him, pity for his wasted promise.

A talented young man unable to achieve his life's dreams while under his parents' control, he may have been prince and rich as Croesus under George III, but a poor little rich boy nonetheless.

He raised his eyes at that point and saw her. Immediately he broke away from the crowd around him and made his way toward her.

"Miss Forsythe, I believe?" He took her right hand in his.

At that point, Lucas melted away in the crowd.

"Your Royal Highness," she said, curtseying deeply. "I am honored."

"We have been awaiting your arrival. I have heard you are the most beautiful woman in London these days."

Anna blushed. "You are too kind, your highness."

"Not at all, not at all." He turned now to a man behind him. "Go get us some of that wretched punch over there, Rutledge."

Anna shivered when she saw Rutledge behind the Prince. The hatred on his face frightened her.

"You know Rutledge?" he asked her as he led her over to the side of the room where several large chairs had been placed for his entourage.

Forgetting to bite her tongue, she spoke honestly. "I regret to say I do, your Highness."

Her words sent the Prince off into gales of laughter. "You are every bit as delightful as we have been told. You do not like him?"

"He has cruelly treated my dear friend from my childhood days. Diana Atwood is the soul of honor, your Highness."

He put a fat finger on fat lips. "Hmm. So you say."

Blood rushed to her face, but she caught herself before she spoke. She had surely already said too much. Out of the corner of her eye she saw Quill enter the drawing room from the back. His cuts had healed some, but not completely. He did not seem to recognize her; in fact, he gave no indication he even saw her.

Anna suddenly wished she could gather up her skirts and run away. Quill would surely criticize her later for having been so forthright with the Prince Regent. But she was not used to dissembling. How could she learn now?

If the Prince asked for her opinion, wasn't she duty bound to give it? She could hear Quill answering that question: she did not have to tell everything she knew. That part of not telling the truth, at least not the complete truth, was only proper. She wouldn't tell the Prince if he had an ugly wart on his nose, would she?

Rutledge returned with two cups of punch. He gave one to the Prince and began to sip from the other. The Prince stopped him before he got it to his lips. "I beg your pardon, Rutledge. That is for my young guest here."

Turning beet red, Rutledge stammered "Sorry," then turned and fled.

Anna envied him that option, for it was not open to her.

The Prince snorted. "He does not own the most delightful manners, that I will allow you." He again tapped his lips with one finger, as though in thought. "You perhaps would not approve my treatment of the Princess."

Anna did not speak. She merely sat still and tried to look demure and humble. As frightened as she was, that wasn't hard.

"Well? Do you?"

"I beg your pardon, your Highness. I do not know enough to form a judgment."

Again he snorted. Anna hoped this interview would end soon. Where had Lucas gone? Would Quill come speak to her? She kept silent, in hopes the Prince would lose interest in her and go away.

Lady Wentworth approached them before too

long a wait. "Your Royal Highness, we are so honored to have you here at Wentworth Place. It is
good of you to honor in this way."

"Quite. You have a charming place," he said,
letting his eyes rove around the drawing room.
"Where is Wentworth? I have not seen him this
evening."

Anna was tempted to point Quill out to him,
but she held her tongue.

Lady Wentworth smiled at him and answered,
relieving Anna of any responsibility in the matter,
"He is seeing to his guests, your Highness. He will
join us soon." She turned to Anna and said in a natural, warm tone, "Anna, my dear, it is good to see
you." To the Prince she said, "May I steal this charming young lady from you?"

"Only if you bring her back before the evening
is over."

As gracious as ever, Eleanor said, "Of course.
Please excuse us, your Highness."

Once they left the Prince, Anna let out her
breath. She hadn't realized she was holding it until
it rushed out of her.

She watched as Rutledge scurried in to join the
Prince. His movements reminded her of a rat, a
rather fat, oily rat. Sweat shone on his brow now,
and his eyes darted back and forth, from one con-
versing group to another. In spite of the heavy
muscles in his hands, neck, and arms, he struck her
as weak. He truly gave her a deep disgust.

Rutledge was whispering behind his hand and pointing, she hoped not at her. By following the angle of his gaze, she learned just whom he was discussing with the Prince—none other than Camilla Drayton-Day.

Camilla had just entered the drawing room. Dressed again in emerald green, but a different dress from the one she wore at Almack's, she looked devastatingly beautiful. Anna's stomach flip-flopped again at the sight of her. Camilla was, in spite of Quill's assertions, a formidable adversary.

Now Camilla was scanning the room to find someone, and Anna knew for whom she was looking.

Camilla's eyes narrowed slightly when she found Quill across the room from her. Then she began a leisurely approach to him. To Anna it looked not at all leisurely, but deliberate and calculated. She wanted to laugh and would have if she hadn't been so frightened.

Camilla was perhaps artificial and manipulative, but that did not make her less overwhelming an opponent.

Lady Wentworth took Anna's arm and began speaking in a casual way to her, telling her small tidbits about different ones of her guests. "Do you know the Chamberlains, Anna? Mr. Chamberlain is, like Quill, new to the House of Lords. He recently inherited his grandfather's baronetcy in Sussex."

Death in Exile

Anna could not keep her attention on Lady Wentworth's conversation. She was entirely taken up with watching Camilla. She felt mesmerized by the young woman's intent. *What would she do next?*

Quill left the guests he had been talking to and approached Camilla with a half-smile on his face that to Anna looked like pleased anticipation. If she didn't know he was dissembling, she would never have guessed.

Quill's look of loving tenderness gave her a pang: she desired all his glances of that nature for her alone!

CHAPTER 23

The next hour was torture. Anna was in the same room with Quill but could not go near him, talk to him, have him touch her. She thought she would soon go raving mad!

And still worse: Camilla Drayton-Day hung on his arm as though she were out on a drunk and needed a lamp post to hold her up. From time to time, her horsy laugh rang out in the room and made Anna feel nauseated. Really, she was the most disgusting creature Anna had ever known.

Thankfully, Lady Wentworth spent as much time with Anna as she reasonably could without neglecting her other guests. Anna knew her purpose was to give the lie to any gossip that Camilla and her cohorts might want to nurture. She deeply appreciated Eleanor's dignity and compassion.

To escape having to return to speak with the Prince, Anna tried to make herself small and inconspicuous. She was gratified to be a nobody: avoiding the *ton's* scrutiny was devoutly to be desired.

At last she noticed a quiet middle-aged couple sitting on the side of the room furthest away from the Prince and his people. The woman, dressed in a plain dark blue gown, her hair pulled severely back, had a pleasant but plain face; the man was quite handsome, dashing even. She asked Lady Wentworth to introduce her to them. "Perhaps they will be protective coloring for me."

Eleanor shot her a look that she couldn't decipher. While it puzzled her, she did not take the time to ask Lady Eleanor what it meant.

She followed her hostess, who stopped once she reached the quiet couple. "Mr. Knight and Miss Austen, may I introduce Miss Anna Katherine Forsythe? She is a young protégée of my family who is not used to such crushes. May she sit here to rest her feet?"

Miss Austen—whom Anna now recognized as the authoress Jane Austen—nodded her head graciously. "Please do be seated, Miss Forsythe. This is my brother, Sir Edward Knight. He has kindly accompanied me here so that I could spend some time with my friend Eleanor Wentworth." Miss Austen's voice was pleasant and musical, her manner patrician yet courteous to one such as Anna, a veritable nobody.

Anna laughed. "I do declare—I may wake up soon and know that I am dreaming. First the Prince speaks to me, and now an even better fate: I sit and converse with Jane Austen." She touched her forehead with her fingertips. "I feel a trifle lightheaded. I am not used to fraternizing with the *ton*."

Jane Austen laughed merrily. "Nor am I. Usually I avoid the public, not because I do not like people, but because I am frequently too busy with friends and family to come to parties away from home."

At that moment a tall, distinguished-looking man approached Jane Austen and Edward Knight. Anna recognized him immediately as the man who had offered Rutledge the letter in which Mathers had incriminated him.

"Mr. Knight, Miss Austen, " the man said. "How are you? I missed you the last time I visited at Godmersham. I'm glad to see you here. How is your guest doing?"

"Our guest?" Edward Knight repeated. His tone was cold, and Anna didn't think he liked the strange man. After a long silence Knight made introductions. "Jane, this is Lyndel Dunstable."

"Lord Basham," he said in correction as he bowed first to Miss Austen, then to Anna. "And this is?"

"Miss Anna Forsythe," Edward Knight answered.

"Your family name is Dunstable?" Anna asked. "Are you related to Matthew Dunstable?"

"Oh, yes, he's my younger brother," he said in an offhanded fashion, as if he were saying Matthew was his bootblack.

"Oh, I see. I met him at Almack's and found him charming."

"Anna Forsythe! Ah. The young woman who turned him into a quivering jelly." He examined her face but said nothing.

Anna figured he was thinking she wasn't much.

"About your guest," Lord Basham said, returning like a dog to his bone. "Is she here with you now?"

"Guest? I'm afraid you have me there," Knight said.

"Diana Rutledge. I heard you brought her here with you."

Edward smiled coldly. "I'm afraid you heard wrong. We have no such guest with us."

Basham flushed, and Anna thought she discerned in him a violent temper, which he was controlling with difficulty. "All right. Forgive me. I must have been mistaken." With that he turned on his heel and made for Rutledge across the way.

When Rutledge saw him coming, Anna could have sworn the man blanched. Did he fear Basham? How were two such unlike people as frigid, debonair Basham and puppyish Matthew brothers?

Quill made his way across the room for Basham and stood very close to him. Anna Kate strained to hear the conversation but missed most of the words. But she did hear the last comment Quill made: "Did you kill Mathers? Here we'd been thinking it was

Rutledge, but it was you all along."

Basham did his best to cover his dismay. "What do you mean? I, kill someone so useless as an old, used-up housekeeper?" He shot his cuffs. "I wouldn't dirty my linen."

At that, Rutledge turned on his old gambling and whoring partner. "You did it and tried to blackmail me over it. I won't let this pass."

Basham gritted his teeth and spoke. "You've basically stolen thousands of pounds from me. Don't forget that." He turned a frozen face away from them and walked off.

Jane Austen watched the whole interchange with a wry smile on her face. Anna looked at her. "Interesting, I'd say," Miss Austen said. Then she dipped her head toward the departing Basham. "What do you think of him, Miss Forsythe?"

Anna flushed and could not speak at first. "I...I don't know him, but he seems odious. I do not care for Henry Rutledge, that oily man next to him."

Miss Jane Austen's eyes widened. "Rutledge? The blackguard who has wronged Diana Atwood?"

"Yes, ma'am." Anna frowned and lowered her head. "But I must not speak out of turn. Forgive me."

"But I asked you." Miss Austen fiddled with the beaded reticule in her lap. "These intrigues are all grist for the writer's imagination, you know."

"You are very kind." Anna now asked Miss Austen earnestly, in a whisper, "You're the people she stayed with, aren't you? How is she now? She is my dearest friend from childhood, and I want to know how she fares."

Edward Knight and Jane Austen exchanged looks with each other. At last Sir Edward said, "Her return to court approaches?"

"Yes, sir, it does."

"She is in better health than she was when she arrived in Kent. Under the circumstances, I hope you will forgive us for not daring to tell you more."

"Oh, yes, sir, I apologize. I don't wish to jeopardize her safety." She twisted her handkerchief in her lap. "I look forward to seeing her no longer under the threat that man wields."

Jane Austen smiled graciously. "As do we all. You know, some years ago, an aunt of ours was falsely accused and taken to court by a shop owner. He was trying to blackmail her into paying him for his silence."

"Oh, my. Dreadful for you all!"

Miss Jane Austen nodded. "It was. But I do want you to know that she was exonerated. She had enough witnesses to her character that the charge was thrown out. And I believe the same result will be the outcome of this upcoming trial."

Edward Knight acquiesced in Jane Austen's statement. "Do have faith in justice."

Anna's eyes teared up. "But Diana came so close to being caught by that man, and so close to being jailed without her friends' knowing so they could speak for her. How many others does this happen to?"

Jane Austen closed her eyes briefly, as though in pain. "Surely too many. But not this time. As Edward has said, hold onto a faith in justice. In a novel, an author can always make the end come out fairly. We must believe that will happen in this case, too, even though this is not a just a story." She leaned across and tapped Anna's clenched fists. "Your friend will come out all right, Miss Forsythe."

Anna scrutinized Jane Austen's face and saw intelligence and kindness in it. "Thank you," she whispered. "Your words comfort me."

Around her Anna began to notice stirrings and whisperings. She looked up to see a panicked look cross Jane Austen's face. The authoress began to fidget more with the reticule in her lap.

"They've noticed you," Edward Knight said.

"I know, and I also know that is why I am here, for them to know I am here. Still," she said quietly, with a rueful smile, "I do not like it. We need to make our good byes."

Lady Wentworth entered their circle and spoke to Jane Austen. "You have graced our party with your attendance, Miss Austen," she said, her voice carrying. "I am so glad you and Miss Forsythe were able to converse for a short time. You will come again?"

"Of course," Edward Knight said with a slight bow to Lady Wentworth. "It has been a lovely evening, but I must take my sister home."

The interchange seemed to be a scene from a play, performed for the benefit of the groups of people standing around the room. It seemed to satisfy them, for they all now returned to their original topics of conversation. Anna heard one elderly dowager say, "So that is Jane Austen, is it? She looks so unassuming. At least she does not make an impression of brazenness, as Mme de Staehl does." Here the older woman sniffed as she spoke condescendingly, "*She* makes quite a scene in public."

A member of the Prince Regent's party was making his way toward them.

"Let us leave, Edward," Jane Austen said hastily. "He will say Prinny wants to speak with me."

Jane and her brother took their leave of Lady Wentworth. "I do not desire Prinny's company," Jane whispered to her friend Eleanor. "If he treated the Princess better, perhaps I would be able to like him better."

Eleanor looked around her, worried that someone might overhear Jane's words. "Oh, be careful! You do not want him to hear!"

"I also do not want him to recognize me. He made me dedicate *Emma* to him, but beyond that I will not go. I do not desire his company."

"Thank you for your care of our friend, Jane. Give Cassandra my best regards."

"I will, my dear. And thank you for your hospitality. You must come again to Godmersham."

With those words Jane Austen and her brother departed quietly, melting through a doorway and into the dark.

Anna had forgotten to be uneasy in the crowd. She turned to Lady Wentworth, a beatific smile on her face. "That was lovely, getting to chat with her. She is quite charming."

"And quite unusual. She seems so ordinary, but don't let that fool you. Ordinary she is not."

"And—she helped me forget Camilla Drayton-Day for a few moments. Thank you for introducing me to her."

Lady Wentworth looked askance at her, then pulled her off into an alcove where they could speak without being overheard. "Did you know our scheme was to get the two of you talking, so people would not believe Camilla's tales about you?"

Anna's mouth dropped open, but quickly she remembered her manners and closed it. "Not really. But why?"

"No one will credit the Drayton-Day now. You are the soul of propriety, and she has Quill's attention. She can no longer spread her venom." She patted Anna's arm. "Stay patient. Once Lucas gets Diana brought back to Mayfair, while Rutledge and the Prince are here, where they cannot spy on Diana, all will be safe, for you and for her."

"Safe. I have definitely not felt safe scrutinized by all these society types. This is most unsettling."

"But only for a short time. Be brave." With that

she turned Anna Kate around and propelled her out of the alcove and back among the company. The force of her hand on Anna's back pushed her right into a tall man in a spotless, well-tailored evening jacket. On the man's arm—it was Quill—simpered that beautiful, hateful green snake, Camilla Drayton-Day.

CHAPTER 24

Quill looked at her and smiled, a cool, formal smile. "Why, Miss Forsythe, it is good to see you this evening. Mother told me you might come." He put his hand protectively over Camilla's, which was resting on his arm. "Have you met Miss Drayton-Day?"

"Yes, Lord Wentworth, I have."

"Oh, yes, at Almack's. I had heard you met there."

You knew we did, Anna thought. *Why the pretense? Never mind—I know why. But I am not made for pretense.* To him she said, "We arrived together in fact, with Toby Esterby and Matthew Dunstable. Miss Drayton-Day was wearing another dashing emerald green gown that night too."

Looking as though she would like to bare her teeth and bite, Camilla's smile was less than sincere. "You are wearing green too," she said. "I never could wear that insipid Nile shade. On you it doesn't look too hideous."

Anna dared not smile, but she felt a twinge of victory. Camilla considered her enough of a threat to be ungracious. *She only hurts herself,* Anna gloated.

Camilla went on. "I see you spent some time with the Prince. He had heard...stories about you and wanted to make your acquaintance."

Her blood chilling, Anna drew herself up. "What kind of stories, Miss Drayton-Day? Did they originate with you?"

Camilla simpered and made a dismissive gesture. "Why, of course not. Whatever makes you think such a thing?" The glint in her eyes, however, confirmed for Anna that the stories had sprouted in that wicked head. A sick feeling filled her: what kinds of stories? More of her being Quill's paramour? The possibility was worse than anything she could imagine.

Quill did not seem to notice the contretemps between the two young women, which was fine with Anna. He would not approve if he knew just how much she wanted revenge on the little witch.

The thought of revenge reminded her of her father: he would be horrified to think she could consider it. He had said living among the *ton* would make her worldly.

Was he right? Was she wrong, being here? Had Papa ever met someone quite as horrid as Camilla Drayton-Day? Perhaps that was his point—she would never have run into someone like her if she had stayed in Andover.

Unless, of course, Quill were to marry the thing and bring her to the Manor.

Anna Kate sharpened her scrutiny of Quill. A shiver of horror ran through her.

His eyes were half-closed, his mouth turned up in his charming sideways smile, as he gazed at Camilla. *He is not pretending! He is drawn to her, more than he has ever been to me!*

Look at me, Quill! She tried to will him to look at her, not at the green snake, but he did not shift his adoring gaze from Camilla's face. Camilla must have read Anna's mind, because at that point she turned her eyes on Anna and smirked. Anna had never seen anyone actually do that, just heard the word. Now that she'd seen it, she hated it.

"I will practice your expression in front of my mirror tonight," Anna said sweetly to Camilla. "I do not know quite how you achieve it."

Uncertainty flashed across Camilla's face. Then, her eyes narrowed and she said through clenched teeth, "Good luck."

Quill clapped both Anna Kate and Camilla on their backs in a chummy fashion, nearly knocking Camilla off her feet. "Now isn't it nice you two are getting along so well?"

Anna took a deep breath to keep from screaming. Just how outrageous would their behavior become before she could escape this triangle?

"Please, my lord," Camilla simpered, "do not

whack me on the back like that. I am not as robust as country girls are."

Quill's eyes widened, but that was the only indication Anna had that he perceived Camilla's barbed comment.

Anna forced a smile, one as genuine as she could manage in the circumstances. "You don't look as though you are very strong. Perhaps you need a tonic. I understand there's a helpful one current with live worms in it."

Quill coughed, then took Camilla's elbow. "We need to move on, Miss Forsythe. It was pleasant talking with you." And then he steered Camilla away.

At that point Lady Wentworth rejoined Anna. "Come with me before the Prince latches on to you again," she whispered. "I believe that before long he and his group will move on to another, livelier party, and you will be forgotten."

Anna was steaming. She imagined smoke pouring out of all her facial cavities.

"Camilla has quite a tongue, does she not?" Lady Wentworth asked.

"Yes, and fortunately for her, my upbringing did not tolerate hair pulling, especially in public. Otherwise that black-haired witch would be hairless."

"My, my, such passion! Come along to my sitting room to cool off." She sighed. "I'm very weary. I will have Randall bring some punch for us both."

She tugged the tapestry bell pull and sat down on a chaise and removed her shoes. "My feet pain me."

Anna began pacing. "Lady Wentworth, you have been the soul of graciousness and kindness to me. I do thank you for that." She held both hands out in front of her in supplication. "I do not understand at all what is going on. Quill is not faking his affection for that...that creature! He really is enamored of her!" She finally subsided and perched herself on a chair near Lady Wentworth's chaise. "I had thought..."

Lady Wentworth closed her eyes. "I am really weary. I do not recall ever feeling quite this way." She rubbed her forehead with her fingers. "He is a supreme actor, you know." She smiled in spite of the fact that her face was contorted in pain. "I...I do not think I can protect you any more tonight. Have Randall get Mrs. Godwin for me. I am ill." Her face was pale and gaunt. "But I need your promise you will not leave this room until Quill says you may."

"Why?"

"Anna, this once, accept what I say and do not argue. Please."

Anna did not answer. She bit her tongue, then crossed to Lady Wentworth and laid her wrist against the woman's forehead. "You have no fever."

"Are you sure? I keep chilling." She grabbed Anna's wrist and pulled her down close so she could fix her eyes on Anna's. "I may not be around once you two are married. He will be good to you. You will take good care of him?"

"Don't say such a thing! You can't be that sick. Hold up—I'll get help."

Lady Wentworth's voice was weakening, but she managed to say forcefully, "No, wait. Do not leave this room alone." She began to shiver, and her teeth chattered so, she could barely get the words out.

"But you are ill! I need to get you some help."

"Randall will be here soon." She lay back on the chaise and did not move for the next few minutes.

Anna continued to sit by her side, holding her hand. Having watched her take care of Diana, Anna knew cool, damp cloths were what Lady Wentworth would prescribe.

It seemed like hours, but Randall finally came in with two cups of punch. "My lady, the Prince and some of his party has left. Rutledge has not, however."

Eleanor nodded. "Thank you," she said in a weak voice.

Anna spoke. "Oh, Randall, her ladyship has suddenly become very ill. Go get Quill. Oh—and Mrs. Godwin. She asked expressly for her. And damp cloths and a ewer of warm water."

Randall's eyes darted across the room at his mistress's still form. "I...I cannot get his lordship. He is otherwise occupied. But I will get Mrs. Godwin and the cloths and water." The imperturbable Randall looked uneasy. "She became ill so quickly." He looked suspicious.

"I don't understand!" Anna wailed. "We were speaking and suddenly she was overcome by her illness. It is a terrible thing!"

"She looks bad. I will hurry."

Anna went back to Lady Wentworth's side. She caught some condensation off the punch cups on a linen napkin and held it against Eleanor's forehead. The amount of moisture was miniscule, but it made her feel she was doing something.

Randall's words hit her. Quill could not come—he was otherwise occupied! Someplace with that green-eyed snip Camilla! Rage rose in her head. Yes, hair pulling would be quite satisfactory at this point, Papa's approval or no!

Outside the door, she heard a commotion. With a backward glance at Lady Wentworth she tiptoed across the room and opened the door carefully. Lady Wentworth had been quite adamant that she was to stay inside the room, but she wouldn't go out, she would merely check to see what the ruckus was.

Once she had cracked open the door, she heard drunken voices arguing down the hall, which was for some unknown reason darkened. In fact every lamp on the first floor seemed to have been put out. She widened the door a bit to see who the men were. She could not make them out in the dark.

Suddenly a dark form hurled itself across the hall and into her midsection, carrying her sideways into the darkened hall, and the door to the sitting room slammed shut.

CHAPTER 25

The force of the blow left her breathless. She could not even cry out. The man put a hand over her mouth, then hissed, "Silence." Because he was whispering, she could not identify his voice.

He didn't smell of bay rum. It wasn't Quill.

Sprinklings of stars spun in her brain. The man's hand covered her nose, and she thought she would black out. She struggled to break free, so she could at least breathe.

Shots rang out on the back hall stairs. The stranger grunted and pulled her into the sitting room and kicked the door to with one foot. She heard the key turn in the lock. Dragging her backwards, he traversed the room to turn off the lamps.

She still did not know who he was, for he was behind her. She wished she could speak, to beg him not to disturb Lady Wentworth.

The man dragged her back across the now-darkened room and settled her in the chair where she'd sat earlier. "Now, Miss Anna Kate, I need your co-operation."

She slumped in relief when she realized it was Toby. She rose from the chair and glared at him. "I think you have broken all my bones. And I couldn't breathe! You rat...!"

"Anna Kate, be silent. You'll ruin the whole gambit. Soon you will learn all, if you can hold on."

"What gambit? I demand..."

Toby put his hand back over her mouth, more gently this time. "Quill always did say you are mad-dening. He's right."

She jerked her head away to get out of his grasp. "What is going on? Where is Quill?"

"He's busy. You need to wait for explanations, Anna. I can't set you straight right now."

"Toby, Lady Wentworth is very ill! You can-not see her in the dark, of course," she said sarcasti-cally, "but she is right over there, on the *chaise longue*. Randall and Mrs. Godwin are supposed to come back with potions and cloths to lower her fever. With all this play-acting going on, how are we to take care of her?" Frustration and rage rose in her voice. "She may die! She spoke as if she might before she passed out. I can't waste time in getting care for her!"

He exhaled audibly. "I didn't know."

Anna's eyes had accustomed themselves to the low light. She could see him running his hand over his hair. No wonder it was always in spikes.

"Man, I don't know what to do," Toby said. "This throws a spanner in the spokes. I can't catch up with him for quite some time."

"At least turn on a light."

"I cannot! Rutledge's men are wandering around the house, trying to find Diana. If we turn on the lamps, they'll be able to see too."

"Diana is here?"

"No, but they think she is."

"Is that good? I mean, is this whole thing a good idea? Who knows what Rutledge and his men might do to this house and to the people in it?"

"Some of Quill's friends are here to control the damage. Once we're through with that gamester, Quill'll have enough complaints against him to lock him up in Old Bailey."

"Or exile him to Australia. That would be poetic justice."

"You have it right there." He grabbed her close. "Hush. I hear something."

Thuds and shrieks filled the house above them. But closer to, and quieter, came the sound of rustling outside the door, then a scrabbling at the knob.

"I hope," she whispered, "it's Randall and Mrs. Godwin. What will Quill do if his mother dies while this fracas tears the house apart?" She struggled out of his grasp. "I have to unlock the door, Toby. I cannot live with the idea of Lady Wentworth getting no aid."

Anna opened the door as quietly as she could.

In the darkened hall she could make out the outlines of two people. They didn't look like marauders to her.

Randall and Mrs. Godwin slipped in, Mrs. Godwin with a kettle of water and some cloths over her arm. Randall had brought a tray; Anna could smell broth.

She took a deep breath. "I'll turn on a lamp so you can see. Stand where you are." She bustled over to the lamp nearest the chaise where Lady Wentworth lay and lit it. She kept the wick low so the light would be fairly unnoticeable. "I don't believe it," she said. "She isn't here!" Putting her hands on her hips, she turned to scowl at Toby. "Just what is going on now?"

Toby flushed. He shook his head but did not speak.

Mrs. Godwin placed the kettle on a small side table with a marble top. "You won't be needing this, will you?"

Anna could smell attar of roses emanating from the kettle of water. "She was here just moments ago and she seemed very sick. Could she have left the room through some other door?" She began circling the room, holding back drapes and knocking on panels to find a hidden door. "Could someone have come in and abducted her?" She put her face in her hands and began to cry. "What if she dies? What if she dies?"

Mrs. Godwin came to her and placed her arm

around Anna's shoulder. "Come sit down, my dear. You have gotten yourself in a tizzy."

Randall said, "Lady Wentworth was looking ill when I was in the room before. But it was horribly sudden, if it was the onset of an illness."

"But she hasn't been looking good lately, and all this carrying on and hiding Diana and then seeing her abducted," Anna said, confused, "and now this stupid party and shooting in the halls at Wentworth Place! Who would credit it? No wonder she is ill! Quill has gone too far."

No one spoke. She examined each one with a riveting look. "Are you all in on this?"

Randall squirmed but didn't speak. Mrs. Godwin looked away and began straightening the cups and saucers on the tea table. Toby turned beet red.

"Randall," she said.

"Yes, miss."

"This is serious."

"Yes, miss."

Anna didn't bother to question Mrs. Godwin or Toby. She felt she would get nowhere with them. As loyal as they were to Quill, she could stick bamboo slivers under their fingernails and learn no more about the plot going on in this house. "I must go." Straightening her mussed dress and hair, she made to leave the room.

Toby darted in front of her to block her access to the door. "No, Anna." His expression was one of bewildered fear. "I have my orders from Quill."

Anna clenched her fists and stomped her feet. "Is that right? So we all have our orders from his lordship, no questions asked?"

He shrugged.

She covered her face with trembling hands. She didn't know whether the trembling was from exhaustion or from anger. Perhaps both. "Why did this infernal game of Quill's have to take place right this moment?"

Shamefaced, Toby shook his head. "I can't say. But you cannot leave this room," he said.

At that moment a second fusillade of shots rang out, right outside the door, upstairs, then belowstairs. Toby cringed, and Anna grabbed the opportunity to kick him in the shins and dash around his hunched-over figure and out the door.

"Anna! Come back!" he bellowed after her.

Keeping her wits about her, she dropped to the floor once out of the room. The acrid tang of gunpowder filled her nostrils. It was pitch black in the hall, for which she was thankful.

Crawling didn't work well. She kept catching her skirt beneath her knees or toes. *I'm sure I managed this better when I was a child,* she thought. *This must be why children are kept in short skirts.*

She could hear Toby muttering behind her. He hadn't dropped to his knees, so she figured he wasn't likely to find her before the lights came back on.

Around her she heard strange gruntings and

moanings, scrapings and shufflings. Mixed with the blackness and the odor, the sounds brought to mind a gothic haunted house. Her skin began to creep, as if in fear of an explosion or earthquake, or even worse, of an unknown hand reaching out and touching her. This was worse than anything she ever imagined, worse than any nightmare.

She had earlier memorized the contents of this hall, that day of her first visit, when she was overly interested in everything about Quillen Rossiter. She knew there had been a candlestick in an alcove about halfway down the hall, between the drawing room door and the back steps. She edged closer to the alcove, then grimaced when she heard her dress rip. Still she kept on toward the candlestick; even though she had no way to light it, she nevertheless resolved to find it.

Rucking her skirts up in one hand, she crawled carefully along the drawing room side wall of the hallway. At last—she felt the edge of the alcove. She stood and scrabbled in the dark for the candlestick.

Just as she touched it, she heard a strange whimpering across the hall. In her fright she nearly dropped the candle. What to do? Did she dare risk giving aid to whoever it was?

Still holding her skirt in one hand and the candle in the other, she crossed the hall. When her knee touched a strange object, she recoiled. It felt like a body.

She put the candle down beside her, close to

hand, then reached out to feel whatever it was she had run into.

"A shoe!" She gasped and sat back on her haunches. Again she heard a ghastly whimper. She took a deep breath, then touched the leg attached to the shoe.

She let out her breath once she realized it was a woman's leg, a very slim one. The silk stockings told her it wasn't one of the maids. "Camilla?" she whispered.

"What?" she cried. "Who is it? Oh—it's you, Anna. I'm so frightened. You won't hurt me, will you?"

Remembering her earlier desire to pull Camilla's hair out, Anna didn't respond to the question. Instead she asked, "Are you injured?"

"Of course I'm injured, you ninny! What do you expect when people race through houses firing off guns and knocking people over? I'm sure I was trampled by fifty men!"

Anna grinned; she was thankful for the dark. "Oh, my. That is too bad." She fumbled for Camilla's hand. "Can you stand up? My hands are full or I would help you."

Camilla tsked. "I suppose. I'm not used to such rough treatment," she whined. "I imagine you are, but I am not."

"No," Anna said, "actually we didn't have many gunfights or stampedes in the vicarage. We were much more backward than you can ever guess." She didn't offer her hand, even though she had dropped her skirts upon standing; the Camilla thing could get up by herself.

"I can't see!" Camilla wailed. "This is dreadful. I will never come back here again, not even if that Quill Rossiter begs me."

"Good," Anna said smugly. "You can stay here if you want or you can follow me. I'm going downstairs to find a light." *And Quill*, she told herself firmly.

It wasn't far to the stairs, she knew. Gingerly she felt her way along the wall; she could hear Camilla snuffling right behind her.

"Are you really hurt?"

"I am sure I am, and I'm sure my hair is a fright. I know I have ladders in my stockings. Oh, and the heel just broke off my shoe!" she wailed.

"Do you cry a lot?" Anna asked coldly.

"Of course not. I usually get my way. What an impertinent question."

Remembering how often she herself had cried lately, Anna softened toward the pathetic creature. In spite of her stunning beauty, in spite of her hateful personality, in spite of the fact she may have the edge with Quill at the moment, Camilla was worth only pity.

She heard a gasp behind her. When she stopped to check on Camilla, the wretch didn't answer. "Camilla!" she whispered. "What happened...?"

At that point a high-pitched scream tore

through the echoing hall. Camilla screamed and screamed and screamed.

"What is it?" Anna growled.

The screaming didn't stop, until Anna Kate reached the girl and grabbed her, only to have Camilla knock her across the face with her arm. "Don't touch me, don't touch me!"

Anna grasped the girl's arms and held them down. Shaking Camilla as hard as she could, she shouted, "Stop it!" in her face.

"He's dead, he's dead!"

"What? Who's dead?"

"I don't know!" Camilla then fell on Anna Kate's neck and began to sob. "There's blood on him, on my hands now! He's dead!"

Then Anna heard a rasping sound, and then felt rough hands on her. Whoever it was wrapped a thick, hairy arm around her neck. "How nice," an oily voice said. "You found her for me, Camilla, pet."

The voice must have shocked Camilla out of her hysteria, for now she took a deep breath and spoke normally. "Don't 'pet' me, you scoundrel. You never told me I would get mussed trying to help you get that simpering wife of yours back. You never told me you'd kill someone!"

"Rutledge!" Anna said. "Let me go." She kicked at his shins, but he twisted away so she never connected.

"Never. I intend to trade for my wife. And who

knows—maybe, Miss Forsythe, you'll see the light of day again once I get her back. Or maybe you won't. You and your pack of friends have caused me too much trouble."

He tightened his grip on her. "Let go, Rutledge," she croaked. "I can hardly breathe!"

He snorted. "Shut up, or you won't take another breath."

He began dragging her toward the front stairs.

Camilla began to screech again. "Wait, don't leave me! I can't stand being around dead bodies."

Anna wondered how many she'd been around to know, but she lost a shoe halfway down the hall so didn't try to ask. Rutledge was breathing heavily in her ear, and she could smell his rotten teeth. She shuddered.

He spoke. "Wentworth and his underlings are in the back of the house, that I know. I wish I could see his face when he learns you're gone."

Camilla began to whine. "Hold on. Why would he care? He pines for me, not this country wench."

"That's what you think, Cam, my pet. He's head over heels for this 'wench,' as you call her."

"Rutledge!" A voice came from what Anna figured was the drawing room door.

"Who wants me?" he snarled.

The next thing Anna knew, she was knocked off her feet when Rutledge went flying across the hall. Someone had given him a blow that would have downed a horse.

Schunk

"What...? Oh, what happened?" Camilla began to moan and whine again.

Anna couldn't get her breath, so she couldn't speak. She wished she could tell the disgusting thing to hush so she could hear.

She heard a scratching noise, then a light flared. She narrowed her eyes against the sudden flash, but she was sure it was Lucas behind the match.

"I'm here, Rutledge, to avenge what you did to Diana." His features were distorted in the flickering light. Even to Anna he looked like a demon from hell.

"You! You don't scare me. You're nothing but a flippin' popinjay!" Rutledge growled as he tried to get to his feet.

Anna held out the candlestick she still held on to. Lucas quickly lit it, and she backed away from the two men so she was against the wall, out of the melee sure to come. Things seemed to move in slow motion as she watched Lucas lean down and pick up a chair leg. The heavy wood had been broken off, leaving jagged spears to skewer anyone who got in the way of whoever wielded it.

"You wouldn't dare, Lucas. You're nothing but a dandy. You can't fight me."

In spite of the bravado in his words, Rutledge's face betrayed him: his eyes were wide with fear and sweat ran down his face. He scrabbled around on the floor to gain a foothold so he could stand and face his enemy.

Lucas swung and hit him in the knees, felling him once more.

"No!" Rutledge screamed.

Lucas hit him half a dozen times around the neck and shoulders. Rutledge groaned and fell on his face. Anna wished she could run away, but she knew Lucas needed her moral support in this horrendous defeat of the horrendous man who nearly killed Diana.

He raised the table leg once more and took a big breath to begin the mighty downswing on the crouching man. Anna's stomach lurched. "Lucas, no!"

He hesitated a split second. She could see the implacable hatred in his face.

"You have the opportunity to kill him, but you must not," she said softly. "You will never be able to claim Diana if you kill him!"

He turned his eyes to her. "Why not?"

"You'll have his blood on your hands, and it will separate the two of you."

She waited as the moment stretched out into what seemed like hours. At last he lowered his weapon a fraction of an inch, and she knew he wouldn't kill Rutledge.

She heaved a sigh of relief.

"Get out of here, Anna," he said coldly. "And take the Drayton-Day with you."

She hesitated, reaching out toward him but refraining from touching him.

Schunk

"I won't kill him. You can leave us. But hurry. Get down to the kitchen."

"Someone's dead back there," Anna told him. "Please see who it is." She shuddered.

By the light of the candle, Lucas showed the battered face of the tall, distinguished man who'd been asking around for Diana.

"Lord Basham!" she gasped.

"Ah, yes," Lucas said. "Rutledge was deeply in debt to him for gambling chits, and Diana wouldn't pay up."

Taking the candle, Anna made her way around Rutledge, who lay breathing heavily on the floor. "You killed him?"

Rutledge merely grunted.

Knowing she'd get nothing from him, she looked for Camilla, who was cringing against the far wall. "Follow me, Camilla." She forced the words out, weary enough to collapse on the floor.

Camilla didn't answer, but Anna heard her shuffling steps behind her. "Here are the stairs," she said. "Take care. You mustn't fall. There are fifteen, I believe."

Once they reached the ground floor, Anna could see glimmers of light behind the baize door leading into the kitchen. She didn't know whether it was safe to go in, but to the kitchen was where Lucas had told her to go.

She bustled Camilla into the kitchen before her. The bright lights blinded her momentarily after the long minutes with no light and then very meager light. When her eyes adjusted, she looked at the group sitting chummily around the large open hearth, feet up on the stonework, large, steaming mugs in their hands.

"Lady Wentworth," Anna said. "And Randall, and Mrs. Godwin. You deceived me!"

CHAPTER 26

Now, Anna Kate—" a familiar gruff voice intoned.

"And Quill!" she squeaked. "Not you too."

He grinned that heart-breaking grin. "Me most of all." His eyes shifted to Camilla. "Why, Miss Drayton-Day, you look as though you've been through a mill."

"You rat!" she shrieked, her cultured tones slipping into broad country ones. "You've shamed me twice! I will never forgive you."

"Does that mean I don't have to worry about making an offer for your hand?"

"I wouldn't give you a drink of water if you were dying in the desert. Of course you may not offer for my hand! I've never been so humiliated in my life."

Quill bowed, a crooked smile on his face. "Whatever you say." He stepped forward to reach for Anna.

"What is going on?" she snapped.

"Now, now. We had to catch him in his wicked design."

"Catch who?" Anna asked, her curiosity getting the best of her.

"Why, Rutledge, of course."

Just then a door Anna hadn't noticed before, built into the wall next to the large stone fireplace, swung open into the room.

Lucas stepped in and gestured to a slumped figure in the doorway. The man was trussed up. He looked searchingly at Anna. "I didn't kill him," he said.

Anna smiled and nodded. "Good for you."

He sketched a bow to her, then spoke to Quill. "He's killed Basham."

Quill nodded. "So now the Beast is out of debt."

Lucas said yes, turned, and disappeared up the stairs behind the door.

Quill walked over to Rutledge and, leaning over, began to pull him into the kitchen so he could close the door to the secret stairs, of which Anna certainly never had any idea.

Camilla scowled. "So you have Rutledge. Can I help you frame that cur? He told me this would be a lark."

"Wrong," Quill said lightly. "Not a lark. And you don't need to worry about framing him. But you did help us catch him in some illegal acts, which we thank you for. Now we can take him to New-gate and good riddance. He's been quite a pain recently," he said as he nudged the unconscious man's boot.

Anna couldn't take her eyes off Quill. He looked more handsome, in black trousers of some rustic fabric and a black shirt, as well as muddy boots, than she had ever seen him.

Lady Wentworth cleared her throat. "Anna...," she began carefully.

With her words, Anna remembered just what she had gone through in the last hour or so. Rage rose in her and she flew across the room, claws extended, to go for Quill's face. He grabbed her arms just in time and deflected her.

"You, you, you...! You planned all this and put me through perdition just for some lark!"

"Lark! What are you saying?" He pinned her arms behind her and crushed her to him. Gritting his teeth, he growled in her ear. "We had to make very sure Rutledge could not wiggle out of these charges. He beat Diana, on top of everything else he did to ruin her, he beat my horse, he left me to die in an abandoned warehouse. And we'd just learned you were next on his list. He was going to abduct you, use you as blackmail to get Diana back, use you for his own vile purposes, and then murder you. Do you think I could allow any of that?"

Anna heard Camilla gasp behind her. She struggled out of his grasp to look at the girl. Her hair was a rat's nest, and her lovely emerald green dress torn into tatters. The twisted grimace on her face did not lend beauty to what Anna saw now was a narrow face with close-set eyes. Why had she thought Camilla was beautiful?

Now Camilla sputtered in self-defense. "How did—? Um, Quill, I had nothing to do with any of that. Don't you go blaming me."

"Oh, you were going to help with abducting Anna. You didn't know about the rest, perhaps, but of your part in the abduction, I am sure." He pulled Anna back closer to him and breathed into her hair. "I won't ever let you out of my sight again," he whispered.

Anna glanced at the others to see if they were watching, but they all seemed to be staring into their mugs. She pulled away again so she could speak. In a small voice, she said, "I'm so glad you're not really sick, Lady Wentworth."

Eleanor smiled at her. This time the smile didn't look quite so elegant; in fact, it looked downright mischievous. "I never told you, did I, that one of our favorite things to do years ago when we visited with the Austens was to put on plays? I did mention Quill is a consummate actor. Actually, risking sounding boastful, I must say I too am quite a good actress."

"We all are," Mrs. Godwin said, "except," she added with a nod toward a blushing Randall, "for Randall. He never could get the hang of it."

Now he blustered, "But I was reared by a vicar, just like Miss Anna, and we neither one of us know how to dissemble." He held his head high. "So there."

Everyone laughed, and the little man blushed even more.

Anna withdrew from Quill's arms, but she continued to lean, ever so slightly, against him. She heaved a sigh of relief. Then she straightened. "Oh! What about Diana?"

At that Lady Wentworth rose. "She is in the ivory bedroom, asleep. Lucas smuggled her in about forty or so minutes ago, with no room to spare. It was so close."

She crossed to Anna and reached out for her hand. "I apologize for frightening you. But you are not a good liar, and if anyone asked, you needed to be convincing that I was on my death bed. And we had to keep you out of the fray. The way you helped to take care of Diana, and then me after she was abducted, told us you would sincerely play the part of the worried friend." She took a deep breath, then pushed the heel of her left hand against her heart.

"You *are* sick!" Anna cried.

"I have a heart condition. After tonight I will swear off all excitement and get rested. I want to be blooming with health when you two get married." With those words she walked regally out of the kitchen, a smiling Mrs. Godwin on her heels.

Randall gestured to Camilla to precede him out of the room. "I will put her in my pantry until the police come."

Schunk

That left only Quill and Anna—and an unconscious Rutledge—in the kitchen. It was warm and Anna was beginning to feel drowsy.

Quill kissed her, and she responded, sweetly and gently. Then she kissed him again, more passionately. As he prepared to return kiss for kiss, she stopped him with one hand raised. "Stop."

"What?" he asked as he kissed her hair.

"I said, stop."

"Oh, what, woman?"

She stepped away from him, placing the deal table between them. "I'm hungry. In fact, I'm ravenous. If you don't feed me, I may have to help myself." She looked around the cavernous room. "Do you have a side of beef? That and a couple of loaves of bread ought to hold me until breakfast."

He began to edge around the table. "How could you be hungry at a time like this?"

She danced lightly a few feet away. "How indeed. I came here, what, five hours ago, with no food on my stomach because I was so nervous I feared I would lose my innards if I had anything in me. Now I'm hungry. So feed me," she ordered, imperious.

"And then what?" he asked, as he reached her and enveloped her once again in his arms.

"Well, then you will either have to propose or face Matthew Dunstable at dawn."

"Pistols for two, breakfast for one?"

She shivered. "That sounds dreadful. Let's don't

pursue that line of thought. Let's think about something nicer."

He kissed her ear. "Like what?"

"A Christmas wedding, you think?"

He didn't answer until he finished kissing her neck. "Need a special license. It's so soon."

She could not speak. Silence reined for a full three minutes. At last she said, "You had better see to it."

At last she disengaged herself from his arms. "You know, I thought Camilla was so beautiful. She didn't look too good after the rout upstairs, did she?"

Grasping her arms, he kissed her nose. "You don't look precisely *de rigueur* right now yourself."

Horrified, she pushed him away. "What?"

"You look almost as bedraggled as you did that day you hid the hogs in the vicarage."

She began to laugh. "You have a terrible memory."

"Terrible! I remember every detail, every tear in that blue dress, every twig in your hair, every smidgeon of mud on your face!" he huffed.

"That's what I mean."

Several days later, Anna Kate interrupted her wedding plans to get ready to accompany Diana, Lucas, and Quill to court. "It's almost like our childhood days," she told Constance excitedly, "when we had outings nearly every day during holiday. Things are almost back to the way they used to be."

"But not quite," Constance added, with a sweet seriousness that marked almost all her speech. "Diana has been through so much, as has Lucas. You and Quill too—no longer mere children."

"No, we are not." Anna smiled. "And that is perfectly acceptable." She ran a comb through her hair, then twisted it up on her head and secured it with tortoiseshell pins. "It's much better this way." She blushed. "Being Quill's wife will be much different from being his friend. And I'm glad."

Soon after Diana arrived in her own carriage. Since Rutledge's incarceration, she had returned to Stafford Hall; her old servants returned also, once they heard the news. Except for Mathers, poor Martha Mathers, whom Basham had killed in hopes of stopping her. He feared her complaints about Rutledge would get the Beast jailed before he could pay Basham back the money he owed.

But those thoughts they all happily put behind them.

"You are glowing, Diana," Constance said. "You look lovely."

Diana bowed slightly and murmured her thanks. "You are very kind."

"I hope you don't mind my asking," Constance continued, "but what will happen to your marriage to Rutledge?"

A look of pain crossed Diana's face.

"I'm sorry. I didn't mean to..."

"No, it's all right." She looked down where her hands kneaded the kid gloves in her lap. "I don't know. I have to take legal counsel about a divorce."

"Oh!" Anna Kate said. "Your packet! I'll be right back." She dashed up the stairs to her room and dug the packet out from the bottom of her wardrobe. She hefted the bag in her hands. A small package, but important.

She returned downstairs and handed the packet to Diana. "See, it's still safe."

Diana reached for it almost unwillingly. "This is what he wanted to kill me for." She opened the drawstring of the bag. "Did you look at them?

"Oh, no, of course not! They weren't mine to look at."

"Hold out your hands." Diana spilled the contents, rubies and emeralds, golden chains and a large yellow diamond.

Anna and Constance gasped. "Oh, my land," Constance said. "That diamond alone must be worth a fortune."

"Yes, sadly. Worth enough to kill for? Not to me." She put the precious stones and chains back into the packet and stuck the whole thing into her own reticule.

"I'll be glad to put them someplace where no one can break in and steal."

"But where is that?" Anna asked.

Schunk

"I'll sell them and build a sort of private village in Andover, for people like your little Travis and her family, where they can go to school and learn a trade. Perhaps then they won't be threatened with poverty and then mistreatment at the hands of people like Rutledge, or the warden that framed them."

At that point, Quill and Lucas burst in the front door with a blast of cold air. Their presence electrified the quiet drawing room where the three young women had been sitting and talking somberly.

Lucas crossed the room and sat on the arm of Diana's chair. He picked up her hand.

"News, Diana," Lucas said.

Alarmed, she arose, pulling away from him. "What is it?"

"It's Henry. There will be no trial. The strain of the past few weeks, the years of hard drinking and rich foods have taken their toll. We just learned he died in jail last night."

The room rang with silence.

Diana raised her eyes to Lucas's; he smiled and leaned down to kiss her forehead. "Oh, Lucas," she said. "Will you marry a widow?"

He stood and paced to the fireplace and then back across the room. All eyes followed him as he walked and pondered this new turn of events. "Will you need to observe mourning?"

Diana, her face alight with hope, turned to Constance. "What do you think the proper thing would be?"

"I think a period of a month will do, then half-mourning for another five or so. You will not seem to be grieving him unduly, nor rejoicing overmuch either."

"That's what my mother said," Quill said.

Diana raised trembling hands to her mouth. "I'm free. I cannot believe it." Anna crossed to her and took her hands. "What will I do with my freedom, dear Anna?"

"Be happy. Just be happy."

"I will not be able to stand up with you, if I observe mourning."

"Hmm. We could put off the wedding," she said, glancing at Quill to see his reaction.

"Like fun we will. We are getting married, woman, at Christmas," he said with mock severity. "I have a seat in the Lords to occupy and speeches to give. You knew that when you met me those many weeks ago in Bond Street. So no wavering now."

Now he sobered. "Bad news. One of the ships headed for Australia—loaded to the masts with poor souls rounded up in that last hunger march—caught fire and burned, just outside of port. All dead." He looked at Diana. "At least you weren't on it. It's going to take time, but I will continue to work for an end to this hideous law. Because the economy is so bad, since Waterloo, there will be more poor folk thrown on the street, and more of them accused of crimes they may or may not have committed."

Anna Kate touched him softly on his arm. "I'm sorry. I'll help you, as much as I can."

Quill looked at her and beamed. Using both hands, he picked her up by her waist and swung her around. "Don't you worry your head about it now. We'll have time after the wedding and after the honeymoon."

"Yes, dear. Isn't he masterful?" she asked the others. Lucas and Constance laughed.

Diana didn't. "Don't be too masterful," she whispered, her eyes wide with remembered cruelties.

The evening of December 24, 1816, Lady Wentworth knocked on Anna Kate's bedroom door in the vicarage. "May I come in?"

"Yes, my lady," she said.

Eleanor entered. When she saw Anna, she began to cry softly. "You are so beautiful. I thought my son would never wake up to the fact."

Anna held her hands out to her.

"That was the reason I was so slow to push for a Season for you. I kept hoping he would propose, but he didn't. So I acted nonchalant, and it almost failed."

Anna laughed. "And here you said you were a great actress."

"I am, but he wasn't paying attention."

The door opened again.

"Papa!" Anna said and flew to her father's arms. His white hair was neatly combed for the occasion, and he wore his best black robe. "My Anna Katherine." Tears filled the pale blue eyes. "You are the image of your mother."

"I am? You never said that before."

"You are. I could not see it until you left me, and then came back." He kissed her cheek, then turned to Eleanor. "It certainly took you women long enough to snare that son of yours."

"That was what I was just telling Anna. He was quite half-witted; I began to despair. But the right ending has been written. Our children will finally wed."

The ceremony was brief. Constance was Anna's matron of honor, Mary her flower girl and Paul the ring bearer. He had wanted Brutus to bear the ring, but Mr. Forsythe forbade the horse to step into the church.

Shades of rose appeared in Constance's and Mary's dresses, in the rose bouquets filling the front of the church, and in small sconces at the ends of each pew in the small Norman church. Cascades of rose and white ribbons graced Anna's hair that Susan had dressed so carefully.

Everyone noticed the shy, tender looks exchanged between Susan and John Bastrop, Quill's coachman. Quill had already given John his blessing to marry her.

Toby stood up with Quill. For once his hair was combed and stayed that way. He had been forgiven for all the mishaps he'd contributed to earlier, with Camilla, and letting Anna escape the drawing room the night of the rout that caught Rutledge in their trap.

And Lucas and Diana sat together, their elbows barely touching. She was still in mourning, but no one expected her to abide by the most stringent rules of mourning: Rutledge had been too big a scoundrel.

Just before Anna began her walk down the aisle, she saw Diana turn to Lucas and whisper something. She knew it was a word of courage to him, that some day they would be standing before the Reverend Mr. Forsythe, right in this very church, to be married too. "By the first of June," Diana said, this time loud enough that her voice carried.

June—the month when all of England burst into bloom. Anna hoped she would be blooming too by then, with the first of Quill's many bright, handsome, talented—and stubborn—children. She could hardly wait.

ABOUT THE AUTHOR

Laurel Schunk has always loved reading and writing. Her first two books are suspense novels, *The Voice He Loved* and *Black and Secret Midnight*. She also has authored two easy readers for second graders. Schunk has a bachelor's degree in French from the University of Illinois as well as a second major, in psychology, from Wichita State University. She teaches writing and likes to encourage other writers. Schunk lives in Wichita, Kansas, with her husband, children, and grandchildren.

OTHER BOOKS BY ST KITTS PRESS

Black and Secret Midnight
by Laurel Schunk

"[Black and Secret Midnight] can be appreciated on different levels—a portrayal of a young girl's coming to grips with the adult world, a study of early-fifties Southern racism, and a good mystery with intrigue, violence, and suspense."

—*The Small Press Book Review*

"This stand-alone story...skillfully mixes a story of segregation in the South and deep, dark family secrets with the plot of Shakespeare's *Macbeth* in a very unique way... This is a very nice first offering from St Kitts Press."

—*Review posted on DorothyL, an email mystery literature conference*

Hyænas
by Sandy Dengler

"Dengler is masterful at creating characters that come alive in any era. I loved Gar. He's so naked—inside and out. Yet at the same time, he is mysterious and secretive. I'm reminded of Ellis Peter's Brother Cadfael series in the way Dengler has placed a unique individual in a unique setting—in a time and place one would least expect to find so astute an amateur sleuth. This mystery buff is already clamoring for more."

—*Pat Rushford, author of the Helen Bradley Mysteries*

St Kitts Press
PO Box 8173
Wichita KS 67208
1-888-705-4887 (toll-free)
685-3201 (local)
316-685-6650 (fax)
stkitts@skpub.com
www.skpub.com/stkitts/

Escape to
St Kitts

**Check our website,
www.skpub.com,
for special offers.**